Blood Stream

C. M. Sutter

Copyright © 2022
All Rights Reserved

AUTHOR'S NOTE

This book is a work of fiction by C. M. Sutter. Names, characters, places, and incidents are products of the author's imagination or are used solely for entertainment. Any resemblance to actual events or persons, living or dead, is entirely coincidental.

The scanning, uploading, and distribution of this book via the internet or any other means without the permission of the publisher is illegal and punishable by law. Please purchase only authorized electronic editions, and do not participate in or encourage electronic piracy of copyrighted materials. Your support of the author's rights is appreciated.

ABOUT THE AUTHOR

C. M. Sutter is a crime fiction author who resides in Tampa, Florida.

With more than forty books published in the thriller and crime fiction genres, she can often be found with a laptop in hand and writing at every opportunity.

She is an art enthusiast and loves to create gourd birdhouses, pebble art, and handmade soaps. Gardening, bicycling, fishing, playing with her dog, and traveling the world are a few of her favorite pastimes.

C.M. Sutter
http://cmsutter.com/
Contact C. M. Sutter - http://cmsutter.com/contact/

Blood Stream
FBI Agent Jade Monroe - Live or Die Series, Book 6

Following a hurricane, the body of a woman with a severely slashed face is discovered in a North Carolina yard. Such a find isn't usually an FBI concern, but when an identical body is located along a Virginia stream, it catches the attention of the Serial Crimes Unit.

Agents Jade Monroe and Lorenzo DeLeon head south, where a monumental task lies ahead of them. With no evidence and no witnesses, they have no way of identifying the victims. A closer look reveals that clues are carved into the women's faces.

The week progresses, more victims turn up in Virginia, and a questionable witness surprises the agents by coming forward. His account turns the case upside down, and the clues begin to make sense.

As Jade and Renz finally close in on the suspect, Jade is blindsided. Only a miracle will get her out alive.

See all of C. M. Sutter's books at:
http://cmsutter.com/available-books/

Find C. M. Sutter on Facebook at:
https://www.facebook.com/cmsutterauthor/

Don't want to miss C. M. Sutter's next release?
Sign up for the VIP e-mail list at:
http://cmsutter.com/newsletter/

Chapter 1

The anchor's comments during the Sunday morning news caught my attention as I sat at the table and enjoyed my breakfast. Already on my second cup of coffee, I craned my neck to catch a glimpse of the scene he'd described.

"Why don't you just go sit in the family room?" Amber asked. "You're going to throw your neck out of joint."

"Nah, I'm not done eating. Those pancakes are still taunting me."

On the TV screen was a pixelated image of a woman who ended up in a North Carolina family's yard after the floodwaters receded from the devastating Hurricane Greta, which had come through the area two days prior. The anchor said the woman's face had been severely damaged, and she would have to be identified through dental records if possible. Many of her teeth had been chipped and broken off, and so far, no one in the area had reported anyone missing.

"Can you believe that?" Amber asked as she took a look at the footage too.

"Believe what?"

Kate had just walked upstairs for breakfast, poured herself

a coffee, and stared at the TV as well.

"A dead woman was found in the receding floodwaters in North Carolina. She actually ended up in a homeowner's yard."

Kate frowned. "Damn. That's disturbing. I hope the homeowner didn't have kids who found her."

I shrugged. "Didn't say. I bet she got caught up in those flash floods and drowned. Poor thing. I also bet her face was destroyed by all the downed tree branches in the water."

"Wouldn't somebody have reported her missing, though?" Amber asked.

I stabbed another pancake with my fork, smeared it with butter, and poured real maple syrup over it. "When hurricanes hit those southern Atlantic states that have so many waterways, it's hard to know where people end up if they do drown. She could have been from a different county fifty miles away. When the rivers flood, they catch houses, trees, animals, and maybe even people as the rushing water builds momentum."

Amber rolled her eyes. "When did you go to meteorology school?"

I waved her off and got back to my breakfast. "Anyway, it's sad, but I bet there will be more missing people reported once everything settles down. That was quite the hurricane."

"And we get tornadoes here but, lucky for us, not much more," Amber said.

Kate raised a brow and huffed. "Says the woman who has never lifted a snow shovel in her life."

"That's what you're for. I do the cooking, remember?"

"Speaking of yardwork," I said.

"Were we?"

I pushed back from the table. "Yep, in a roundabout way. Kate, take your pick. Mowing or weed whacking?"

"I'll mow."

"Good enough. Then let's get started. We've got a football party to attend this afternoon."

Chapter 2

Chris slowed the Jeep to a stop along the edge of the muddy lane. The only interruption to the quiet was the nearly dry back-and-forth squeaking of the windshield wipers. The rain had all but ended. After killing the engine, Chris stared out the driver's-side window. Confusion set in since nothing looked the same as it had five days earlier. The hurricane had disrupted everything, and the area was littered with upended trees and debris.

After pulling up the hood of the rain slicker, Chris climbed out and cautiously looked up and down the lane for signs of people anywhere then slogged through the mud. Each rubber-booted step made a *squish*, the mud sucking them in like wet concrete.

Only a week earlier, small streams had veered off the main Roanoke River. They were now unidentifiable. Everything was a tangled mess of brush, and the stream was thirty feet beyond where the bank used to be. All of the waterways ran together.

I can't even tell where I left her. I hadn't planned on that damn hurricane, and now I don't have any marker or reference to go by.

Chris had hidden Lorraine Tilley beneath an old fallen tree along the bank, where she would never be found, but now the tree was gone too.

Who would have thought a hurricane that was predicted to wreak havoc on the Gulf Coast states would come up the East Coast and flood all the rivers here instead?

Chris continued on until water from the overflowing stream trickled into the rubber boots. Lorraine was nowhere to be found, and the fallen tree seemed to have floated away.

Damn it. She has to be here somewhere, maybe caught in tangled limbs. I'll come back in a day or two when the water recedes and look again.

Chris returned to the Jeep, pulled off the muddy boots, and tossed them over the seat. Several more names remained on the list, and time was a factor. Those people would have to be addressed within the next few days. That night was as good as any to strike again, and going forward, all of the bodies would be dumped farther away from the main river, possibly even weighted down with a rock.

The drive home to South Boston from the dump site would take twenty minutes. Later, Chris would put the plans for Deena into motion then think of a better place along the river to leave her body. The Roanoke River was the best choice since the water teemed with wildlife. Its course ran hundreds of miles from Virginia through North Carolina until finally emptying into the Albemarle Sound along the Atlantic Ocean. Dozens of rivers, streams, and creeks branched off the main river, providing a slew of options to work with.

Dumping her closer to Roanoke is the smart thing to do. Nobody in law enforcement will connect the dots, especially since I left Lorraine more than two hours from there. The hurricane damage and searches underway will keep everyone good and busy for the next week. The best time to complete my mission is while everything and everyone is out of sorts.

During the drive home, Chris imagined a half-dozen scenarios of how the attack would go down. Deena would answer the door, stare into an unfamiliar face, and ask the typical question, "May I help you?"

Then Chris would strike. Deena would take a few seconds to process who the person at the door was and why they were there, and that was all the time Chris needed. The hit would be fast and efficient—no wasted time, energy, explanations, or apologies. Blindsides were the only way to go. Anything else could get messy, and messy took time. Deena would be down within seconds, dragged through the garage and out to the back of the Jeep. After that, the rest would be easy. All that mattered was dumping her in a well-hidden spot where she couldn't float away.

Hours passed, then it was finally time. Deena was about to participate in her own death just by answering the front door. Later at night wouldn't work. As a single woman, she would be cautious and likely wouldn't open the door. Any woman with half a brain wouldn't answer a knock after dark.

Chris had the necessary items already in the Jeep. Too many would be cumbersome, and all a killer really needed was one weapon and the element of surprise. That and that alone would do the trick, but it didn't hurt that Chris had also taken kickboxing classes several years ago.

It wouldn't get dark until eight o'clock, providing plenty of time to do what was necessary and take Deena to the chosen stream that branched off the river. There was no chance of Deena floating away like Lorraine might have. That stream was only twenty feet wide, and the area was heavily wooded. Nobody ever went fishing there since it was impossible to cast without the line getting tangled in low tree limbs. Chris had previously checked the area and found a game trail only twenty feet from the overgrown dirt road that led to the stream—or what remained of it. Years ago, it was wider, but logjams and beaver dams had slowed the flow of the fast-moving water. There were plenty of other streams and branches of the river to fish in, so Chris wasn't too concerned about Deena ever being found. That spot would be perfect.

At six thirty, Chris arrived at Deena's home. Luckily, she lived in a sparsely populated area without immediate neighbors. The police would have nobody to question as possible witnesses—if they ever found out who Deena actually was. As with Lorraine, her face would be unrecognizable, her phone would be destroyed, and her purse would be taken and buried.

The lonely road had no traffic, making Chris's job easy. Homeowners looked at those types of neighborhoods as bonuses that afforded them privacy. The homes were on streets and country roads that real estate agents used to their advantage by listing them as premium secluded locations for discriminating buyers.

Chris chuckled, took the sidewalk to the front door, and

pressed the doorbell. The sound of shoes getting closer confirmed that Deena was definitely at home. Because of her recent nose job, Deena likely had one more day of seclusion before her new reveal, but she would never see tomorrow—or any other day for that matter.

The door opened, and Chris, dressed as a delivery person, held a bouquet of flowers.

"Oh my word!" Deena's smile looked like one of genuine happiness, and Chris knew why.

"Deena Norman?"

"Yes, that's me."

"Sign here, please."

"I can't believe he sent me these flowers. My birthday is coming up. I just love him so much!"

Chris chuckled. "Points for the hubby, right?"

"No, I'm not married. I'm sure they're from my boyfriend, though. What a sweetheart."

Chris kept a firm grip on the bouquet—one less mess to clean up—and passed the signature capture pad to Deena. That was the moment to strike. As Deena looked down, her hands occupied, Chris kicked her in the stomach with lightning speed and sent her flying backward. The kick knocked the wind out of the unsuspecting homeowner. Deena lay on the floor in a fetal position, writhing, grunting, and gasping for air as she held her abdomen. One more strike would completely disable her, and the petrified look on her face said she knew it was coming. She couldn't even ask why before a boot came down on her face.

Chris stared at the outcome. Deena's teeth were crushed,

some lying on the floor next to her, and her new nose was pushed to one side. Blood ran from her mouth, nose, and left ear. She wasn't dead yet, but she would be soon enough.

Chris knelt at Deena's side and whispered, "I hope you can hear me. I want to look in your eyes and see what fear looks like. You have to know that I'm about to kill you. You brought it on yourself, of course, and even death is too good for you, but it is what it is. Killing you is the only way I can right the wrong and get over the pain that you and the others have put me through. Now, with whatever strength you have left, whatever life remains in your body, I want you to look at me." Chris looked into Deena's eyes and watched her lids flutter with the little amount of life that remained in her body. "Good. Now, let's get this done, shall we?" Chris was about to end Deena's life but paused. "Hmm… I think I'll let you suffer just a little longer. God knows I've suffered for months."

To inflict more pain, Chris made a few cuts here and there. They would have to do for the time being. Blood from the new wounds ran onto the tile floor beneath Deena.

Chris stood, walked to the utility room—making sure to avoid the blood—and filled a bucket with hot soapy water. It was time to clean up the mess, flush it, then remove Deena from the house. Back at Deena's side, Chris casually picked up the fragments of teeth, washed the pool of blood off the floor with a sponge, then flushed it all down the toilet. The blanket found in the linen closet would do just fine. Chris wrapped Deena in it, dragged her to the garage, then pressed the button on the wall and waited for the overhead to lift.

With Deena jammed into the back of the Jeep, it was time to go, but first, Chris returned to the house, grabbed the woman's phone and purse, locked the front door, and retrieved the flowers and signature pad. With a final look around to make sure nothing had been missed, Chris took the remote from Deena's car, grabbed a bowling-ball-sized rock from the flower bed, and placed it in the back next to the body. Once finished, Chris climbed into the Jeep, lowered the garage door, and drove away.

The drive to Deena's final resting place would take a half hour, and if Deena wasn't dead by the time they arrived, Chris would finish her off. The face still needed more cuts, then Deena would be dragged to the stream, put in the water, and held down with the large rock taken from Deena's own yard.

After finally reaching the dead-end road, Chris killed the Jeep's engine, climbed out, and opened the rear door. Inside the rolled blanket, Deena let out a faint moan.

"Still alive, are you? You're tougher than I thought you'd be."

Chris opened the blanket and pulled out a pocketknife. There was work to do, and Deena's face, although puffy and a sickly shade of dark blue, needed to be unidentifiable. After making a dozen slashes from Deena's forehead to her chin, then carving her cheeks, Chris stood back and took a look.

"There, that's better, but now, you need to die."

With a swift slice across her neck, the job was complete. A few gurgling sounds was all that was left of Deena Norman.

Dragging Deena's body to the stream was much more of a struggle than Chris had anticipated. The tangle of brambles on the forest floor, along with a week's worth of rain and hurricane damage, had made the ground farther inland just as wet, slippery, and treacherous as the spot where Lorraine had been left. By morning, though, the fish and woodland predators would be well-fed.

Tomorrow, Chris would look for Lorraine's body for the final time. That morning's search had proven useless. Lorraine was likely gone, which made Chris think even more about the body that had washed downstream, through the reservoir, then ended up in that family's yard. It had to be Lorraine. There was no other explanation.

I haven't seen anything on TV about that body since last week, and they sure aren't going to describe her or show her face on the news. It's unidentifiable anyway, so I guess it doesn't matter if it's Lorraine or not. The cops have no way of knowing who she is, and Drew sure as hell isn't going to report her missing. Maybe I should change up my routine. Two dead women in the water may indicate too many similarities, especially if Deena is found. I've got three to go, and I'll make sure to dump each of them in a different environment, maybe even in a different state. West Virginia isn't far from Roanoke, and that might be the smartest way to go.

Back home, Chris ate a late supper then took to the computer. Looking for a dump spot for the next victim was crucial. There was only a week left and three more people who needed to die. It would be an ambitious task to complete, but if anyone could do it, Chris could. Payback and hatred were the great equalizers, someone had once said, and there was plenty of each to go around.

Chapter 3

Monday, August 29

A smile crossed my face while on my way to work. My mind took me back to the preseason football party we'd hosted a week ago and all the parties we would enjoy for the entire football season. That party was the first one Amber, Kate, and I had hosted, but it wouldn't be the last. We were on a once-a-month rotation. The preseason games were insignificant to us, but hanging out with our dearest friends took precedence over the games we didn't particularly care about. Everyone in our group, let alone the state, was a diehard Packer fan, and that would never change. In a few weeks, the Packers would play two of our biggest rivals—the Vikings and the Bears. I would have to find out who was going to host those parties, but no matter who did, the parties would be a blast. Next weekend, Jack was hosting a Labor Day barbecue, so I hoped there would be no requests that took us out of town, as my weekend social calendar was filling up fast.

I had no idea what was in store for us that day but would

find out soon enough. It was a new week, and as far as I knew, we would all remain in the area since I hadn't heard of any serial crimes in our region—or any neighboring region—that would require our help.

Over the last week, the only thing I'd seen on the news was the hurricane updates along the southeast coast. There had been great damage both statewide and on the local level, a lot of flooding, and lives lost. I wondered whether I would ever be able to live in the South. Hurricanes scared the heck out of me, and as much as I loved the southern charm and genteel culture, I wasn't fond of stifling humidity all summer long either. Every state had its pros and cons. Living in Wisconsin meant winter started early and ended late, along with daily gray skies during those months, something else I wasn't fond of. I wondered where the perfect place to live would actually be.

Looking a half mile ahead out of my windshield, I saw nothing but brake lights. The daily bottleneck was coming up. With all the never-ending freeway construction, I marveled that none of those engineers had yet figured out a way to eliminate that problem.

I glanced at the clock then mentally calculated how much time it would take to get to St. Francis once I made it through the logjam.

I wouldn't call the office unless I was sure to be late. Someday—I'd been saying for several years—I would buy one of those converted warehouse condos in Milwaukee's Third Ward like Taft had, but the prices had increased dramatically over the last few years. Also, crime in Brew City was off the charts, nearly as high as in Chicago. I had to admit my procrastination was likely because I loved my home, my city, and my roommates.

With my fingers crossed, I was able to get through the traffic jam and arrive at our headquarters with six minutes to spare. I stood in front of the retina scanner, waited as it scanned, then passed through the door. I entered my security code on the next door's keypad then headed for the elevator. Our third-floor offices were only two minutes away.

When I walked into our shared office, Renz grinned. "The woman who likes living on the edge." He glanced at his wrist. "With thirty seconds to spare."

I swatted the air. "Shush. I made it before our shift officially begins, so that's a win for me."

"Sure, if you say so. No time to power down and sip a relaxing cup of your favorite beverage after that long drive before we dig into another workday."

"Whatever." I chuckled. "I'm used to living on the edge. Nothing hair-raising is on the books for the week anyway."

Renz pushed back his chair and stood. After a stretch that nearly popped the buttons on his shirt, he headed for the door.

"Quit your diet?" I teased.

He frowned and looked at his stomach. "Why? Am I gaining weight?"

I grinned. "Only you would know. It's just an observation." I followed him out the door. "Maybe you should start taking the stairs every day instead of the elevator."

We entered the conference room and took our normal

seats. I did a quick head count. Other than Taft, it looked like all our agents were in attendance. While we waited for our boss to arrive, everyone made small talk and shared news of their weekend.

The clacking of Supervisory Special Agent Maureen Taft's shoes was unmistakable as always. She wore low-heeled dress shoes every day, and they had a distinct sound. Our boss was coming down the hallway.

"Good morning, Agents."

We responded in unison then remained quiet while Taft organized her notes.

She looked up, smiled, and began. "Mike and Carl, you'll be leaving this morning for Wichita, Kansas. Our help is needed there. In recent days, there've been four child abductions. The children aren't related, apparently don't know each other, or live in the same neighborhoods, and their ages range from five to twelve. The city police as well as the Sedgwick County Sheriff's Office have been working the disappearances nonstop for days. They've just called in the local FBI, and they've requested our help." She slid folders across the table to both agents. "Brief yourselves during the flight. A driver will pick you up in Wichita, then you'll meet with the group who have set up a war room at the police department on Main Street. Any questions?"

Both agents said they were good, picked up the folders, then left the meeting.

Maureen continued. "We're having local problems, as you all know. Crime in Milwaukee is out of control. The rest of you are going to pitch in to help the Milwaukee police in combating the unprovoked attacks on everyday people walking the streets of downtown Milwaukee. Two people died last week after being bludgeoned by total strangers as they made their daily walk from parking garages to their offices. Smash and grab is one thing, but to stick around and beat victims to within an inch of their lives, and two of them not surviving, is extremely disturbing. We need to find out if those perps are unrelated individuals or if they're working as a group and prosecute them to the fullest extent of the law. If the city doesn't resolve this situation soon, all of you might be putting in overtime."

I knew that meant working weekends, but I remained stoic and didn't give away my disappointment.

Taft glanced at the clock. "Head out now and meet up with Captain Fields at the State Street police station."

With six of us, we needed to take two cruisers. Renz, behind the wheel of ours, pointed the nose north, and Kyle followed us. The drive would take less than fifteen minutes since the morning rush hour had ended.

Just after nine o'clock, we reached the police station. Renz pulled into the parking garage attached to the multistory building.

Inside the station, after showing our credentials to the officer behind the plexiglass wall, we waited for the captain. It took only a few minutes for him to come out, greet us, and ask us to join him. His team of nine detectives and thirty day shift officers were brainstorming, he said, but so far, nothing had stopped the senseless attacks and murders in the city.

The six of us joined the group and introduced ourselves,

giving a brief history of our backgrounds. After that, the captain updated us on what had and hadn't been addressed so far.

"We have three suspects on video at two of the attacks but none at the others. They could be the same people in both attacks, but the footage is grainy, and they were all wearing hoodies. Their size and mannerisms seemed the same in both cases, though."

"But no facial shots at all?"

"Unfortunately not."

"Is there enough TV news coverage?" Renz asked.

The captain sighed. "It seems so, but nothing has led to any arrests. Actually, none of the tip calls have proved credible."

"And are there more cops on the street since these attacks began?" I asked.

"Our district is the entire downtown area, so every available officer, day and night, is walking and patrolling every street. The problem is we can't be everywhere, especially when some of the attacks happen in parking garages."

I couldn't even recall the number of times I'd walked through parking garages, and they always gave me the creeps, especially when I was alone at night.

Kyle took his turn. "Is there a pattern? Certain times of day, days of the week, or a particular street or area of downtown?"

The captain lowered the roller map of the downtown area where the attacks had taken place.

"Honestly, and as bad as it sounds, there haven't been

enough attacks to get an average. A dozen attacks don't seem out of the ordinary in today's world, but when two of those innocent individuals ended up dead in a week's time, well, that's too many in my opinion."

"Understood," Kyle said.

"Why don't we go through the days and times the attacks happened, and then your detectives can tell us if there were similarities in the murder methods, how the victims were found, evidence gathered, and then what your department has done so far," Tommy said.

Fay, with a pen and paper in hand, jotted down everything as it was told to us.

A knock on the door disrupted our joint brainstorming session, and Captain Fields called out for the officer to come in.

"Sorry, folks. This shouldn't take but a minute. What's up, Officer Kent? I hope to God it isn't another attack."

"No, sir. I'm actually supposed to ask Agent DeLeon to call his supervisor immediately."

With a puzzled look on his face, Renz excused himself to go make the call to Taft out in the hallway. Out of courtesy to the group, we had all powered down our phones during the meeting.

Renz returned a minute later and said that he and I had to leave. My eyebrows shot up. It was clear that a case somewhere else needed our attention, and there were still four very capable FBI agents who would work with the police to solve the attacks in Milwaukee.

After handshakes and apologies, Renz and I left the police

station. Once outside, I asked why Taft had called us away.

"Not sure of the details, Jade, but it looks like we're heading out today."

"Where to?"

"Somewhere south. That's all I know so far. Taft will fill us in when we get back to the office."

Working for the Serial Crimes Unit of the FBI was my job and my passion. I had known it would take me out of town a lot, but I was still disappointed that I might miss the weekend events back home, and I often did. Of course, I wouldn't share those feelings with Renz. It was the price of being in the FBI, and I was proud to be a senior special agent on our team.

We were back at our St. Francis headquarters at ten fifteen, and as we exited the cruiser, I gave Maureen a call. She said to come directly to her office for our briefing.

"So no information except south?"

Renz shrugged as he waited his turn to use the retinal scanner.

"I wonder if it has anything to do with the recent hurricane."

"Doubt it," he said. "That responsibility is on the state and FEMA."

"Yeah, that's true."

We took the elevator then two hallways before we reached Taft's office. Renz knocked, and she invited us in.

"Make yourselves comfortable while I go over the assignment with you." Maureen pointed at the guest chairs, and we sat down. "So, I don't know if either of you saw that news segment last weekend about the horrible flooding caused by Hurricane Greta along the Roanoke River."

I nodded as Taft spoke.

"There were casualties in several states throughout that region. The Roanoke runs between Virginia and North Carolina and then out to Albemarle Sound with the Atlantic Ocean just beyond that. That river is four hundred miles long with many creeks, streams, and lakes that branch off it."

I had no idea where she was going with the story, but we were definitely getting a geography lesson. Then I remembered what I'd seen on TV on Sunday morning.

Maureen continued. "There was a segment on the news about a family finding a dead woman who appeared in their yard after the floodwaters receded. Nobody has come forward to identify her"—she slid photos across the desk—"and this is probably why."

I grimaced when I stared at the image of the badly damaged corpse. The photos showed a waterlogged body blackened by bruises, I assumed from being in the flooded river and bouncing off every tree, log, and rock she had floated by. Deep cuts and scratches covered every square inch of visible skin, especially her face.

Renz spoke up. "So we have an unidentified dead woman who wasn't reported missing from who knows where, who likely drowned in the floodwaters. Where do we come into play, and why?"

Taft looked concerned. "Well, it turns out that after the autopsy was completed, the coroner said that the woman's teeth were pulverized, something that shouldn't have happened by floating through water, and her cuts were smooth and consistently the same depth and length. If she were cut up by tree limbs and debris, then the injuries would be ragged and inconsistent. Finally, she didn't have water in her lungs. Then, the most concerning and shocking thing in the autopsy report was that she likely died several days before the hurricane even made landfall."

I was stunned, and that meant we had a killer on our hands who'd used the hurricane to their advantage. Still, it wouldn't warrant the FBI getting involved.

"With all due respect, Boss, why would the locals call the FBI on an isolated case with a victim whose identity and home location are unknowns?"

With her index finger, Taft tapped the photograph. "Because there's another body in Virginia that looks exactly like this one."

I turned to Renz and silently mouthed the word *shit*.

Chapter 4

By noon, we were comfortably seated on a commercial flight bound for Durham, North Carolina. I took the window seat simply because I loved that escape, even if it was only for a few hours.

After taking off and hitting our cruising altitude, as we passed over the landscape beneath us, I wondered where all those nearly invisible roads led, who lived in the area, and what their lives were like. I saw large and small cities and wondered what towns they were and if they were good places to live. I'd always had a sense of wanderlust, but because I wasn't born with a silver spoon in my mouth, my only way to see other cities and states was usually through my job.

"Someday."

Renz tapped the back of my hand. "You thinking out loud?"

"What? Oh, I guess I was. Just wondering."

"About?"

"About our huge country and the enormous number of people who live in it. What are they doing? Are they happy? Do they live in a wonderful community with dozens of friends?"

He chuckled. "Sounds like fantasyland. Nobody lives a perfect life, Jade."

I nodded as I stared at the beautiful cloud formations and the sun's rays piercing them.

"So why did you say someday?"

"I was just thinking about a vacation. I'm overdue." I gave him a quick smile. "But we all are."

"That's for sure, but for now, we better go over our notes so we can hit the ground running when we get there."

"Right, but with two bodies in two different states, how are we going to work that angle?"

Renz huffed. "Hell if I know. The first body found was the hurricane victim, and that's in North Carolina. We're landing in Durham, and Taft said that was about an hour from the location the victim was found at. We'll have to work them like individual cases, and then when we have the information we need, we'll try to connect them and see if something makes sense."

"Yep, that sounds like the only way it'll work."

After going through our notes, contact names, and a list of places to stay, Renz and I had lunch then leaned back for a half hour of shut-eye. After cases in the past had kept us up all night, catching a nap now and then was a bonus that we wouldn't pass up. We had to stay fresh and be present while doing our jobs.

I set the alarm on my phone, gave the landscape one more look, then closed my eyes. The next thing I knew, my phone was buzzing in my pocket, and I couldn't believe a half hour had passed. Quietly and with my bag in hand, I slipped out past Renz, who was still sleeping, and went to the restroom to freshen up. I finger combed my hair and grinned when I remembered the warning my mom had always given me. "Jade, never use a brush on your curls, or you'll end up looking like an orangutan." Mom had always had a way with words, but they sunk in. Each day, I used either my fingers or a pick. I dabbed powder on my face to cover the sheen, brushed my teeth, then applied a fresh coat of lip gloss. I was ready to get our rental car and drive to Henderson, the town nearest to where the body was found that had a branch of law enforcement. There, we would meet with the people who'd requested our assistance.

Back in my seat before we landed, I nudged Renz. "Hey, we'll be on the ground soon, and I thought you'd want to freshen up."

After yawning, Renz rubbed his eyes. "Yeah, good idea. I'll be right back."

I looked out the window again. The city was coming into view, its rolling hills in the distance. I'd never been to Durham, but from the online images I saw, it looked like Brightleaf Square was a great restaurant and shopping area. It was a shame that we wouldn't have time to check it out. At times when visiting wonderful places I wished I had a man in my life, but for now, having good friends kept me happy.

Renz returned to his seat just as the landing gear was being lowered. It would only be a few minutes before we touched down.

Once we landed and the plane taxied in, I checked the local temperature on my phone—eighty-four sunny degrees, not unlike the weather we'd left in Milwaukee. I smiled knowing my go bag was packed with the right clothes.

We deplaned and headed downstairs to the car rental area. Tory had already set us up with a midsized sedan. All we needed to do was pick it up and be on our way. Once we touched base with our contact at the sheriff's office in Henderson, we would follow the deputy out to the location where the Jane Doe was found.

"I imagine we'll head there right away after meeting everyone, don't you think?" I asked.

Renz nodded. "Yeah. Better to do that while we have plenty of daylight left."

We got our car, and while Renz programmed Henderson's sheriff's office into the navigation system, I made the call to Deputy Alan Rice, who would be our liaison while we were in North Carolina, and told him we should arrive in an hour. After hanging up, I called Taft to let her know we had landed safely and were on our way to Henderson.

I gave Renz a glance as he drove. "So, we won't get too much accomplished today. Go to the scene, review the reports and read the interviews the deputies took, and then?"

"And then find out what has been done so far. Forensic testing, evidence gathered, if any, and so on. We'll read the autopsy report, too, and speak with the coroner if he's still on duty. If not, we'll do it tomorrow."

"Sounds like plenty for our first day here considering the time. We'll check into our rooms, drop off our bags, then discuss the case over supper."

I sat back and intended to enjoy the next hour. I loved to

rubberneck, especially in locations I hadn't been to before. Once we arrived in Henderson, everything would be strictly business.

After leaving the populated Durham area and heading north toward the border of Virginia and the more rural regions, I watched the scenery pass by. Small houses surrounded by woodlands dotted the landscape. North Carolina was full of trees, and around the small towns, it seemed there were far more green areas than homes.

We reached Henderson at five fifteen and easily found the sheriff's office on Church Street. A town of fifteen thousand people wasn't hard to navigate. Renz parked, and we headed up the sidewalk.

"I wonder which way," I said.

The sheriff's office was grouped with the courthouse and the administrative offices.

Renz pointed at the nearest building. "Let's go find out."

After passing two deputy cars, I figured we were heading the right way. We entered the building, and Renz walked to the counter.

"Excuse us. Is the sheriff's office in this building?"

"Yes, sir. You've come to the right place."

"Good." Renz pulled out his bifold ID wallet that contained his badge. "Deputy Rice is expecting us."

"Sure thing, Agent DeLeon. I'll let him know you're here."

Renz gave her a friendly nod, and we sat in the lobby to wait.

Soon, we heard a door open and close and the sound of

footsteps coming from the corridor. A man who looked to be in his mid-thirties, dressed in the typical tan deputy's attire, walked over and introduced himself as Alan Rice, a seven-year deputy in Vance County and our liaison during our stay in the area.

We shook his hand and followed him through several hallways until we came to the sheriff's office.

"We've grouped up in our cafeteria. Hope you don't mind, but it's the largest area we have for more than a half-dozen people."

"That's fine," Renz said. "So, who are we meeting with?"

"Sheriff Crane is in attendance, two other deputies, one who went with me to the scene, and our county medical examiner."

"Sounds good, and we're very interested in the coroner's findings."

Deputy Rice looked over his shoulder at me. "Yes, ma'am. It's a real mystery."

Seconds later, we entered the lunchroom, where four people sat with a carafe of coffee centered on the long folding table. Deputy Rice made the introductions, and we took our seats.

The sheriff, Donald Crane, summarized the events that had unfolded since a week ago Saturday after the 911 call came in.

"It was around nine a.m. when we got the call from the Woodworth area. The family, Mr. and Mrs. John Greenley and their teenaged kids, had gone outside to assess the damage after the floodwaters finally receded. According to

John, their dog began barking incessantly, and they walked over to investigate. That's when they discovered the body." He let out a long sigh. "I understand you've come from Milwaukee, and I don't know if that information showed up on any of your news stations, but the media got wind of it, followed our team to the site, and took their own pictures using telephoto lenses. Sensational news like that doesn't happen often in our area, and by Sunday morning, the footage was all over the news stations in the Southeast."

I nodded. "I actually did see the segment that Sunday morning too. Thankfully, the image of the woman was pixelated. I'd imagine since the hurricane and all the damage and flooding it caused was still ongoing, the media jumped on that piece about the unidentified woman. A dead body ending up in somebody's yard would be big news no matter where the location was."

"I guess so."

Renz took his turn. "So, Rice and Moore were the first deputies on the scene?"

"That's correct, Agent DeLeon." Sheriff Crane tipped his head toward Rice. "Go ahead and take it from when you and Moore arrived."

Chapter 5

As we listened closely, Rice relived his account of last Saturday morning. He and Deputy Moore had arrived at the Greenley home at a quarter of ten. The ME, Conrad Leto, and his assistant, Liam Mayes, pulled in behind them, and the forensic van came in last.

"The ground was still pretty soggy, and we had to be careful not to get stuck. Everything was covered in thick mud and debris. We sidestepped the waterlogged areas as we made our way to the front porch and up to the door. Mr. Greenley came outside and directed us to the body. He had placed a sheet over the woman to keep the vultures from pecking at her."

I grimaced at the thought, and those photos we'd seen earlier came to mind. The poor woman was in bad-enough shape without opportunistic birds making an easy meal of her.

"Everything comes off the Roanoke, you know. Our nearest water source is the Kerr Reservoir, which is part of the river. I imagine the woman came from upstream, into the reservoir, then since every stream flooded, too, she ended up in the Greenley's yard."

"She couldn't have floated farther?" I asked.

"No, ma'am. That branch ends right there. That's why they had so much debris in their yard."

"Understood," Renz said. "And Dr. Leto, can you summarize what you thought when you saw Jane Doe?"

"Certainly. I will say that a field exam is an assessment and nothing more. I never base my official report on that, especially if a body has been in water for some time. The findings are far from accurate. She was badly bruised, cuts and scrapes everywhere, waterlogged, and severely bloated. I don't want to be too graphic, but she literally had to dry out a bit before I could see that her cuts were smooth and uniform, not at all like one would get from downed limbs scraping against skin. It wasn't until the woman was on my table, cleaned and dried, that I could give her injuries a closer look. By the amount of decomp, too, even without her being in water, I'd say she died several days before the hurricane. Plus, she didn't have any water in her lungs."

"So we heard. Does that mean you suspect foul play?" I asked.

He shrugged. "There's nothing else it could be unless she died naturally outdoors and when the flooding began, it swept her away."

"Natural death at what approximate age?" I asked.

He shook his head. "Early thirties."

I gave Renz a quick glance. My gut was leaning more toward the coroner's assessment, foul play, especially since Taft had said a second body in Virginia was found in the same condition.

"Then you do know about the similar case in Virginia, right?" I asked.

Rice spoke up. "Sheriff Crane said that was why you were called in. The information came across the wire of an unidentified woman who might have died from a drowning. Because the Roanoke River is so large and goes for such a distance, all that information, especially when the victim is unidentified, is shared between counties, and in this case, because of the hurricane and the proximity of the river, it was shared between states."

I addressed the coroner. "Have you and the medical examiner in that area exchanged findings?"

"We have, Agent Monroe, and because that female didn't have water in her lungs either, and was approximately the same age, we concluded that not only were the cases similar, they were identical. Those women were killed by the same person."

The hair on my arms stood up. "So, the Jane Doe here died first, correct?"

"She did. I'd say over a week ago. According to the ME in Roanoke, his Jane Doe died a few days later."

I rattled my fingers against the table. "You could give a relatively accurate description of her, though, right? Hair color, eye color, height and weight. Tattoos or notable scars? Even the clothing she had on?"

"Yes, of course."

"Good. That'll definitely help. Can you put that together for us to have by morning?"

"Not a problem, Agent Monroe."

I continued. "So, the river runs west to east, but I guess that doesn't help us much. The perp could drive from any starting point to Roanoke and place the body in the river."

Sheriff Crane agreed. "And therein lies the problem. We have no idea who those ladies are, where they came from, or where the killer lives."

"Where exactly was the second body found?" Renz asked.

"In a remote spot along a shallow stream near Green Hill, Virginia. That area has several offshoots from the main branch of the river."

"Remote area? Then how was she discovered?" I asked.

The sheriff responded. "Apparently, a man was scouting out fishing spots but realized the area where that stream was had too many trees along the shoreline. Nowhere to cast. As he turned to walk back to his truck, he caught a glimpse of something yellow snagged in the low-lying trees. He walked over to investigate and saw her body. A large stone had been placed on her abdomen, a way to keep her submerged, I'd assume."

I blew out a breath and checked the time. "What do you say we head out? We'd like to give the Greenley's yard and the area leading to it from the river a closer look."

"You bet." Deputy Rice pushed back his chair and stood. "I'll lead the way."

I nodded a thanks.

"We'll reconvene in the morning, say around nine a.m.?" Sheriff Crane said.

Renz headed for the hallway. "That sounds good."

Chapter 6

Rice had warned us to stay close behind his car. The long and poorly maintained back roads were still muddy and full of potholes.

At the intersection of Rock Springs Church Road and Antioch Church Road, we made a left onto a narrow gravel path. I jerked my head to the right and looked over my shoulder. A mailbox stood where we'd made the turn. "I guess this is a driveway. We must be there."

We had arrived. We were at the home of John and Clarissa Greenley, and it was seven o'clock—much later than I'd hoped. Even though the thick tree cover cast more shadows than I would have liked, we still had an hour of daylight left.

"Good thing we didn't drop off our bags yet," I said as Renz parked next to the deputy's car.

"Yeah, why's that?"

"Because unlike you, I don't intend to traipse around in the mud with my good shoes on. I always pack lightweight rubber boots."

"That's great. Then you can do all the traipsing."

I frowned. My tough talk didn't go the way I had planned.

We exited the car at what appeared to be a small mini farm devoid of neighbors and walked with Rice to the door.

"John is expecting us," Alan said. "I talked to him during the drive."

Renz pointed his chin toward the porch. "Good enough. Let's see what he has to say."

The dog's barking must have alerted Mr. Greenley. He stepped out to the porch, greeted Rice, and waited for our introductions. Once that was taken care of, Renz began.

"So, Mr. Greenley, we'd like to see where you discovered the body."

"Sure thing. Right this way."

We walked with the homeowner along the side of the house and down to the shed.

He pointed just beyond the building. "Normally, the stream runs parallel to our property about a hundred feet beyond the outbuildings, but the flooding caused by the hurricane brought the water right up to the edge of that shed. It took a couple of days before the water receded enough for us to even head down there, but when we did"—he wiped his brow as if reliving that moment— "well, that sight isn't something I'll soon forget."

"I'm sure it isn't." I looked around, and the stream was about fifty feet beyond the shed. "Is that where the stream normally is, or is it still high?"

"It's got another few days before it'll be back to normal. It peters out back in the woods. Along my property is where this small branch ends." He sighed. "Looks like there's a big jam of brush to clean up."

"Is it too squishy to go back there, say, even halfway?"

He shrugged. "That's up to you, but I doubt that you'll find anything. It gets pretty tangly down there where the water ends, and it's always muddy but even more so now."

"Mind if we just look around the yard a little, then?"

"Nope. Fine with me."

Renz spoke up. "Do you recall how many days the water level stayed high? Before it began to recede, I mean."

"Hmm…" John rubbed his chin. "A couple of days and then two more days to reach the point it's at now."

"Okay, thanks."

I wanted to ask more, but John wasn't a professional, so his account would be anecdotal and nothing more. We had the coroner's and deputies' reports, as well as the Greenley's original statements, to look over again. Whoever that woman was had died more than a week ago and likely spent several days in the water as the river and streams flooded their banks and carried her as far as she would go—the Greenley home. We would reconvene in the morning and get the detailed description of the woman from Dr. Leto. Airing her face on the news would be impossible because of how she looked, but we could describe her, the clothing she wore, and the general area where she was found. We had nothing to work with other than the obvious—that somebody had wanted her and the second woman dead.

I returned to the car, slipped on my boots, and took to the yard. I didn't wait for Renz to tell me where to go or what to look for. Since I was the designated traipser, he'd said, I was taking charge of that task. From the house, I walked until the tips of my boots were submerged in water. I could see nothing on the ground beneath the water's surface anyway, and so far, I hadn't found a single thing that might have come from the victim—or signs that somebody had placed her there, a scenario that I doubted. I walked parallel to the water until it ended then turned around and went the other way along its temporary bank for a quarter mile. There wasn't a shred of clothing, not a single shoe or anything that said she'd gotten tangled in the brambles. She'd simply floated along until she got beached on a patch of clear ground, and that was where she remained until she was discovered. There was nothing else there to look for. I returned to the car, tossed my boots into the trunk, and slipped on my other shoes. Back at the house, we thanked Mr. Greenley, climbed into the car, and followed Rice down the long driveway to the main road.

"Well, what do you think?"

Renz glanced my way. "About what?"

"Taking a couple of hours out of the afternoon to go out there and back."

"I think that time could have been put to better use. We didn't learn anything, did we?"

"No, not really. I didn't find anything either."

"Too much time has passed since she was discovered. Chances of finding something in the yard were slim. What I'd suggest is that first thing in the morning, we get that description from Dr. Leto and put it on the news stations within a hundred-mile radius. I doubt that any killer would drive a body farther than that to dump it, and the locations where Jane Doe One and Jane Doe Two were found were closer than that anyway."

I agreed. Something needed to kick-start the investigation. Other than the sheriff's office and coroner taking care of the preliminary work they would normally do when a body was discovered, nothing else had moved the case forward.

"Should we take a look at the body ourselves?"

"I think so. We need to know if most of her injuries came from a weapon and, if they did, how many cuts there were. Also, if the cuts were situated in one specific area."

I groaned. "I know one thing."

"What's that?" Renz asked.

"From the pictures we saw, and if all those cuts were from a knife, it looked like somebody really wanted to destroy her face."

Renz gave me a concerned glance. "And that's something we have to find out from the coroner in Roanoke too. We need a copy of their Jane Doe's examination report and autopsy findings. Before we travel to Virginia, I want to make sure there's no doubt that we're dealing with the same killer."

Back in Henderson, we said good night to Rice and drove to the hotel Tory had booked for us on the edge of town. It was a newer-looking place with an attached restaurant, and that was a plus in my book. We planned to check in, clean up, then enjoy a much-needed supper in the restaurant.

After checking in, Renz and I parted ways at our second-floor rooms and agreed to head downstairs in forty minutes. The restaurant looked to have a decent menu and was open until eleven o'clock.

With my hair twisted up in a clip, I hit the shower. There wasn't time to wash my hair since it would take hours to dry.

I would address that task tomorrow night. The streaming hot water pelted my tired muscles, and it felt good. With the washcloth and soap, I scrubbed the day's humidity off my skin. After drying off, I was reenergized and put on clean clothes—the same clothes I would wear tomorrow. As I sat on the edge of the bed, I made sure there weren't pieces of grass or clumps of dried mud on my shoes before I slipped them on, and there weren't. I grabbed my purse, phone, and room key then walked next door to Renz's room. I gave the door two raps, and he answered immediately. I liked a guy who was ready to go on time, and Renz was always prompt.

"Shall we?" I asked. "I'm starving."

"Same here." He pocketed his key, and we took the hallway elevator to the main floor.

Inside the restaurant, we were seated by the hostess. Several couples and a family or two were still enjoying their meals. It was time to relax, meaning no shop talk. We would make our plan for tomorrow in the morning over breakfast. At that moment, I just wanted to eat, have a few glasses of wine, and talk about anything but dead bodies.

After a wonderful supper and a promise to invite Renz to our next football party if we weren't out of town, we said good night and parted ways at our rooms. The plan was to head down to breakfast at seven forty-five then go directly to the sheriff's office. From the hotel, it was only a five-minute drive.

I was exhausted, but that was normal on a traveling day. Tomorrow, we would have a better grasp of the case, get copies of everything we needed from the coroner in Roanoke, too, and bring up the suggestion of airing Jane Doe's description on the news throughout North Carolina—and maybe even Virginia. Since the second woman was found in Virginia, there was a possibility that both women came from somewhere in that state.

Before I dozed off, I made a quick call to Amber. Wisconsin was an hour behind North Carolina, so I knew she was still up.

"Hey, sis," I said when she answered.

"So, what's the word?"

I let out a tired sigh. "Nothing yet. We just gathered information today, but there is a twist to the investigation."

"Really? More than the coincidence of you investigating the death of that woman we saw on TV last Sunday morning?"

"Yep, even more than that."

"Go on."

"Not only is there a second woman in Virginia who died mysteriously, but according to Taft, her body was in the exact same condition as the one here in North Carolina."

"Meaning the damage to both of them wasn't caused by bouncing off downed trees and being scratched by limbs?"

"Nope, and according to the coroner, the body here didn't have water in her lungs, and she was actually dead before the hurricane even hit the coastal states."

"Wow, that really is a twist. So somebody killed her and possibly the second woman and then dumped them in the river?"

"Something like that, but as time goes on, we'll learn more."

"Hmm. Does that mean you're going to miss Jack's Labor Day barbecue party?"

My groan spoke volumes. "I really don't know, Amber. We have less than a week to solve this case if I plan to join everyone for chicken and ribs on the grill. Damn, that sounds good."

"Well, get some sleep and then kick your detecting into high gear. You didn't reach senior special agent status for nothing, and Renz is a kick butt agent. Between the two of you, you'll figure it out."

I chuckled. "Thanks for the vote of confidence. I hope we can live up to it. Night, Amber."

"Night, sis."

I hung up and plugged my phone into the charger. Tomorrow would come soon enough, and I needed to put the case to rest so I could get some sleep. I fluffed my pillow, got comfortable, and shut off the light.

Chapter 7

The shrill alarm nearly jolted me out of bed. Still tired and disoriented, I squinted and wondered where the heck I was. Then reality kicked in—it was Tuesday, and I was in a hotel room in Henderson, North Carolina.

"Oh yeah, we're on a case."

I gave my phone a closer look to make sure the alarm had gone off when it was supposed to. Another half hour of sleep would feel wonderful. I groaned when it showed seven o'clock, the time I had set. "Damn it."

I tossed back the blankets and stumbled to the bathroom. A splash of ice-cold water to my face would make me coherent enough to prepare coffee in the hotel's small four-cup pot.

With that done and the coffee brewing, I turned on the TV to the news station that came in the best. The weather report was on, and it looked like a partly sunny day with high humidity was ahead—a repeat of yesterday. I returned to the bathroom to start the drudgery of making my face presentable. If I had my way, I would work in my pajamas, never wear makeup, and keep my hair in a clip and piled on my head, but as an FBI agent who was supposed to represent, I couldn't get away with looking anything but clean, refreshed, and business casual, day or night. With the washcloth, I soaped up my face then rinsed and dried it. I applied a small amount of sunscreen then foundation and a pat of powdered blush. A few coats of mascara and I would be fine until I drank my coffee and brushed my teeth. Then lip gloss would finish off my look.

I dressed as I watched the latest international news, then an update on the economy, and finally, what was going on in Durham and the surrounding area. I downed two cups of coffee then checked the time. I would be knocking on Renz's door in ten minutes. With that, I shut off the TV, brushed my teeth, and applied lip gloss. I grabbed my phone and briefcase, pocketed the key card, and left the room.

Renz opened his door just as I was about to knock. "Good timing," he said as we walked to the end of the hall and boarded the elevator.

In the restaurant, we ordered off the menu. The line for the continental breakfast was long because the man in charge of making omelets was backed up. Two eggs over medium, bacon, hash browns, toast, and orange juice would tide me over for the day if necessary, and of course I had plenty of coffee. Renz ordered a stack of pancakes, two eggs, hash browns, and an order of sausage. We were good to go. While we waited for our food, we planned our day.

"First, we should view the body, see the description Dr. Leto put together of her, then get in touch with the Roanoke coroner. We need the same reports and photos from him that

Dr. Leto is providing us so we can compare bodies. After that, we'll see what Taft wants us to do about the news stations. If she thinks it's a good idea, then we'll coordinate everything with the sheriff and possibly do the same with the second Jane Doe in Virginia."

I blew over my coffee then took a sip. "So in a sense, we'll be giving ourselves a head start on the Virginia woman?"

"That's right, as long as the cases are undeniably related. Compare autopsy reports and descriptions of the women, and if everything is eerily similar, we'll get in touch with the law enforcement agency in the jurisdiction where she was found and discuss the chance of getting her on the news too. Those women can't be nobody. Somebody has to know they're missing, somebody has to care, and somebody has to be related to them."

I raised a questioning brow. "One would think."

Renz tipped his head toward the waitress carrying a big tray and coming our way. He rubbed his hands together. "Looks like our breakfast is here."

I glanced at the people still standing in line for their custom-made omelets and grinned. "We'll probably be done and gone before those poor people get to eat."

"Speaking of eating, let's get a move on. We're meeting everyone in thirty minutes."

After enjoying our delicious breakfast, Renz and I headed out. We had plenty to keep us busy that day with all the contacts we needed to make. I wasn't sure when we might move on to Virginia, but my gut was telling me that everything originated there. What was most important was finding out who those women were. That information could lead us in the direction of the killer and finding out why he'd chosen to murder them in the first place.

We entered the sheriff's office at 8:50 and showed our credentials, and the deputy behind the counter said we could go on in. Everyone was gathering in the lunchroom, just like yesterday.

Renz and I continued on and, once inside, saw that the same group of people were already seated and talking among themselves. We exchanged hellos and sat down.

Sheriff Crane opened the meeting by saying they had gone through the reports of all the missing people in a three-county area but nobody matched Jane Doe's description.

I frowned and wondered how they would know what she looked like when her face was unidentifiable. If they were going only by height, weight, and hair and eye color, I couldn't see how they could discount anyone who fit those parameters. A person's face—along with other distinguishing features such as tattoos or noticeable scars—usually confirmed the identity of a missing person. I shot Renz a concerned glance, and he noticed. I knew he would address their methods, so I kept quiet.

"Excuse me, Sheriff Crane, but without a positive ID of a face, tattoo, or unusual scar, how can you be sure any woman who has been reported missing and whose height and weight are similar isn't the right one?"

Crane rubbed his chin. "I understand where you're coming from, but there were only five women who went missing in those three counties, and none of them were five foot three and one hundred twenty-two pounds. They were all at least twenty pounds heavier."

The sheriff had a point. Whatever our victims weighed when they met their fate wasn't likely to change by twenty pounds after death.

I turned to the coroner. "Dr. Leto, can Jane's weight fluctuate at all after death?"

He shook his head. "Only if animals got to her and ate parts of the body. The only evidence of that were fish nibbles, and they weren't significant."

We couldn't dispute the sheriff's statement. None of those five missing women were Jane Doe.

I spoke up again. "I think we should check the missing persons database for all of North Carolina and Virginia."

Crane looked at Renz, and Renz nodded. "I second that. It's our belief that both women might have been from Virginia. Jade and I are going to take a look at Dr. Leto's description of our Jane Doe, then we'll compare that to the description of the victim found in Virginia. We'll need the contact information for the county medical examiner there who conducted the autopsy."

Dr. Leto passed me the hard copy findings for Jane and offered to make copies of what the other coroner had sent him.

"We'll need his phone number and email address too," I said.

"Not a problem, Agent Monroe. I'll get that off my laptop right now."

A half hour later, Renz and I sat alone in a vacant cubicle

and reviewed the autopsy and descriptive findings for both women. They were close in approximate age according to the medical examiners. North Carolina Jane Doe had blond hair, and Virginia Jane had brown. They both had blue eyes. Neither had identifying features like tattoos or scars, although the Virginia Jane had pierced ears. Neither had on jewelry when found. They were similar in height and weight, give or take an inch or two and a few pounds. Neither had water in her lungs, and both had slashes everywhere but primarily on the face. Their teeth were destroyed, and the manner of death for both was a slash across the neck.

I leaned back and groaned. "Those women went through hell before they died. I just hope the slashes to their faces were done postmortem."

Renz placed the coroner's photographs side by side. Once again, I grimaced at the sight, and now there were two of them. The face of Jane from Virginia was just as cut up as the face of Jane who lay in the morgue here in North Carolina. The slashes on their bodies were as smooth and uniform as if the same knife had been used over and over again, but the facial cuts were somehow different. The similarities were obvious, so I pointed out the differences.

"Renz, look closer at the faces of both women. Most of the cuts are vertical lines like on the rest of the body, but what are these?" I pointed at the cheeks of both victims. "Those cuts are different. There are horizontal and what even look like curved cuts on their cheeks."

Renz lifted one photo then the other. He held them only inches from his face. "I think you're right, Jade, but all of that bruising makes it hard to see them. We need to capture those marks alone without the interference of the other cuts or the discoloration."

"Is it possible to virtually erase everything else?"

He shook his head. "I'm not sure, but we're going to find out."

"What do you think it means, or does it mean anything at all?"

"Don't know, but we have to talk to the forensic team. Since we're going to Durham anyway to view the body, let's pay the crime lab a visit too."

Renz made a quick call to the coroner in Roanoke, introduced himself, and explained that we were going to try to segregate images of the cuts on the women's cheeks from those of the rest of the facial slashes. Something about them looked different, but we needed to drive to Durham and ask the forensic lab there if they could help us out. We were excited to hear that the coroner said their crime lab was in the same building as his office. He would ask them if that was possible and text Renz right back. If it was, they'd do it on their end and send the photographic attachment to my email address. Renz thanked him and ended the call.

We walked to Crane's office and told him our findings and what we planned to do about them. Either the cheek cuts were some kind of symbols, or they were nothing but doodles created by a sick psychopathic killer.

It was time to head to Durham. Dr. Leto offered to meet us in the lobby and said we could follow him back. We needed to view the Woodworth victim's face up close and personal to see if we could make out anything.

After parting ways in the parking lot, we climbed into our car and followed the doctor out of Henderson. I made the call to Taft then set my phone to Speaker.

Chapter 8

"Hey, Boss," I said as soon as Taft answered. "I have my phone set to Speaker so Renz can join in on our conversation."

"Good. Are you two making any headway?"

I looked at Renz to see if he wanted to take the lead, but he pointed his chin at me to go ahead.

"Well, yesterday we went out to the site where Jane Doe was found, but with it being a week since her discovery, we didn't see anything useful. We've reviewed all the documents and compared the coroners' reports, and they're relatively similar. As we speak, Renz and I are driving to Durham to get a look at Jane Doe in person. We've noticed something unusual on both women."

"Really? What's that?"

Renz took over the conversation. "Actually, Jade noticed it. Both victims have multiple slashes all over their bodies, and they all go vertically, including most of the cuts on their faces. But when you look at their cheeks, the pattern is different."

"In what way?" Taft asked.

"It's hard to explain, but there are more horizontal marks

and even curved cuts in that two-square-inch area."

"Hmm… that is odd."

"And both women have them, which makes it even more odd. I spoke to Dr. Finch in Roanoke, and he said the crime lab was in the same building as the morgue. He said he'd go ask the techs if there was a way to virtually erase all the other facial cuts so we could get a better image of the cheek markings."

"That sounds like a great idea. Anything else?"

"What about airing the descriptions of both women on the news here and in Virginia?"

"Not a bad idea either, Jade. See what you can find out about the cheek cuts and then call me back. We'll make a decision then."

"Sounds good, and we'll talk later." I clicked off the call and stared out the window. We were passing a road sign that said it was ten miles to Durham. I hoped to get answers that day. If not, then we would review all of the missing women reports that had come in over the last two weeks in Virginia and North Carolina. No matter what, we needed to learn the names of those women and why they had met the fate they did.

Minutes later, Renz's phone buzzed. Since he was driving, he handed it to me.

"It's a text from Dr. Finch. He said the forensic lab can virtually eliminate all the cuts on both women's faces that aren't on their cheeks and lighten the bruising so what's left is easier to see. He'll send the revised images over within the hour."

"Great. I'm interested to see what we have left. Either those cuts will be something we can decipher, or they won't make sense at all."

I was excited to see Jane in person. Under normal conditions, I could literally live without viewing bodies, but oftentimes we had to, and in this case, it could give us helpful information.

The blinker on Dr. Leto's car flashed for a right-hand turn. Renz followed him into the parking lot of a two-story tan brick building. The doctor parked in a space that had his name on a placard, and we parked in a visitors' spot right behind the doctor's car then climbed out.

"Would you like to speak with our forensic team now or view the body first?"

"The forensic team in Roanoke said they could take care of getting us those images, and Dr. Finch is emailing us the virtual changes. We should have the images soon."

"That's good news, and it'll speed things up." The doctor opened the door and allowed us through. "Right this way to my office. It won't take but a minute to prepare Jane for viewing."

We followed him then waited in his office while he disappeared into the morgue and autopsy area.

My shiver was involuntary. It happened every time I stepped into the medical examiner's area of any building. The air was always cold, and the thought of dead bodies lying in refrigerated drawers gave me goose bumps anyway. As a law enforcement professional, I should have been used to that sort of thing, and I was, but it didn't mean I couldn't be sad, angry, empathetic, or even question the next phase of our investigation after a heart stopped beating.

"Agents?"

Renz and I snapped out of our thoughts and looked up at Dr. Leto.

"Jane is ready if you are."

Renz glanced at me, and I nodded.

"Let's do this." I stood and, with Renz at my side, walked toward the doctor.

We entered the refrigerated storage room, where one drawer had been pulled out and the body bag unzipped. A badly damaged Jane lay exposed with a disposable sheet covering her nude body. Dr. Leto stepped aside and allowed us room to walk freely around her and inspect what we needed to see. The unusual cuts to her cheeks were even more noticeable as we stood barely inches from her face.

"Dr. Leto, do you have any small pieces of cloth or tissue I can cover the rest of her face with?" I asked.

He walked to a counter and brought over the tissue dispenser. "Will these work?"

"Yep, thanks." I covered everything but her cheeks then took pictures as close as I could to her face without blurring the image. I called Dr. Leto back over. "In your opinion, Doctor, were these injuries"—I pointed at her cheeks—"cut with the same knife as all the others?"

"I believe so, and it isn't a large hunting type of knife. If anything, I'd say it's smaller, likely something with a foldable six-inch blade."

"So a pocketknife?"

"Yes, a knife like that."

"Can you tell if the cuts were done in stages, layers of sorts?"

"It seems so, as if all the vertical cuts were done first, and possibly as an afterthought, the others were done on her cheeks."

I glanced at Jane's hands, arms, and chest. "Did you see any defensive wounds?"

"None whatsoever. She was either near death or at least unconscious when she was cut."

I wrinkled my face. I would never get used to the cruelty and madness killers were capable of, but that was why they were killers. They lacked the empathy gene and a sense of guilt. They didn't care about right or wrong. They did what they did because they enjoyed killing or they hated the victim so much they had to kill. Some of them wanted to kill because of simple curiosity—they wanted to see what dying was like for the victim and what killing was like for themselves.

"All the darkened skin can't be from crashing into things in the water, can it?" Renz asked.

"No, but much of it was. Once she was out of the water, she began to deteriorate, causing her skin to rot in a way. Keep in mind, summer water is warm, not icy water, which could have preserved her. I'd say she was beaten or at least handled roughly by her killer, too, before she died."

I'd seen enough and looked at Renz. "Anything else you want to ask?"

"No. We'll look over your pictures and the ones sent from

the forensic team to see if we can make anything out of the cuts on both women's cheeks. Other than that, there's really nothing else Jane's body will tell us."

I nodded. "Okay."

We thanked Dr. Leto and showed ourselves out. In the car, I logged into my email account to see if the message and attachment had come in from Dr. Finch, and it had.

"We need to go somewhere, print out the revised images along with the pictures I just took, and then review them."

"Sure. Let's find a library."

I did a search on my phone and found a library only six blocks away. Renz headed in that direction. All we needed was a good printer and a quiet place to study the pictures.

Chapter 9

Carrying everything we needed inside with us, Renz and I headed into the library and straight to the counter. We asked about printer usage and were told that printers were stationed by every group of study tables. The cost was fifty cents a sheet. We thanked the woman behind the counter and looked for a table where no one else was seated.

"Over there on the far left," I whispered.

As soon as a group of women and children with art supplies walked through the front door, Renz and I made a beeline for the table.

Once there, I tried to make use of every square inch by spreading out paperwork, my briefcase, my laptop, and whatever folders happened to be in my briefcase. It wasn't because I was being selfish, but we needed room and some privacy.

I took a seat, opened my laptop, then clicked on the attachment Dr. Finch had sent. Renz scooted his chair closer and nodded.

"Let's see how the images look."

I quickly glanced to my rear to make sure there wasn't

anyone sitting behind us who could see the laptop and the horrific images, then we leaned in and stared at the screen.

I whispered to Renz, "Wow, it almost looks like letters carved into their cheeks now that the bruising is lightened up and the other slashes have been taken away. I'll zoom in the best I can and then print it out. You got any change?"

Renz stood, dipped his hands into his pockets, and came up empty. I shook my head then riffled through my wallet.

"I only have twenty-two cents and a couple of tens. A magnifying glass would be helpful too."

"What do you suggest?"

"Go ask the librarian for change and see if she has a magnifying glass we can borrow. Do you have any singles?"

Renz pulled out his wallet and looked. "Yeah, I've got a couple of bucks."

"Good." I pointed my chin toward the counter. "Then go ask."

I watched in amazement as Renz shuffled away. Why men never wanted to ask for help dumbfounded me. When it came to asking how something got assembled, how to get from point A to point B, or whether they could borrow something, men turned into piles of mush. I believed they thought that asking questions would destroy their image of being all-knowing about everything under the sun. I chuckled to myself and opened the gallery on my phone, where the pictures I had just taken of Jane were stored. I looked up as Renz walked toward me.

"She had change in her purse, but they don't have a magnifying glass."

"Okay, whatever. We'll stop at a store on our way out of town and buy one if we feel the need for it. I've got to figure out how to get my phone and laptop to recognize that printer so we can use it. Why don't you go ask—"

"Nope."

I huffed and got up. "Fine. I'll do it myself." I walked to the counter and told the librarian that I needed to use the printer but the images would be coming off my phone and laptop. She explained how to connect to their printer, I thanked her, and returned to the table. After following her instructions and printing out the sheets, I placed the three images of the women on the table—two that Forensics had improved and the one of the North Carolina Jane from my phone. I turned over the sheet with the cell phone photo so we could focus on the two women. We needed to compare their similarities and differences since Forensics had made identical changes to both pictures. At the top of each sheet, I indicated which woman was in the photo. On the one on the left, I'd written N. C. J. D., and the one on the right had V. J. D. Since their faces had been completely destroyed, we had to correctly identify each woman. Also, the Jane found in North Carolina had been dead several days longer than the Virginia Jane.

I groaned. "It sure would have helped if either of them had had identifying marks on their bodies or at least teeth that were intact."

"Don't think the pulverized teeth was an accident. The killer wanted to make sure the women couldn't be identified. Destroying teeth and their faces was the best way to do that."

"Right, but how would the killer know if the women had scars or tattoos? Not everything is obvious when a person is fully clothed."

Renz raised a brow. "You're right about that, and unless the killer was intimately familiar with each woman, there wouldn't be a way to know. I doubt that dumb luck came into play. The killer is too cunning for that."

"Okay, let's focus on these images. We can speculate later. Let's compare the left cheeks to each other first to see if anything about them looks the same." I took the copy of the Virginia woman's photo and placed it on top of the photo of North Carolina Jane so their cheeks would be side by side. "I'm thinking these cuts either spell out something from left to right, they're initials, or they're gibberish meant only to throw us off if the women were ever found."

"So you have what could be an *L* or an *I* as the first cut."

"That's correct." I jotted that down on my notepad and felt like we were playing a macabre word-find game. I looked at the picture on the right to see if the first cut was the same, and it wasn't. "What do you make of yours?"

"It could be an *O* or a *D*."

"Do you think the cuts on one woman's face continue onto the other? Maybe spelling out a message?"

Renz shook his head. "I haven't got a clue, but I think we'll go crazy trying to figure it out."

I slid the sheet showing the Virginia woman's face back toward Renz. "Okay, you work on her face while I do the same with this one. We'll write down every letter we think we see on both cheeks and then compare the results."

Renz looked around. "Do you want to do that here or go back to the hotel, where we can talk freely?"

I followed his eyes and realized the library was filling up. "Damn it," I whispered. "We don't want to lose our focus, Renz."

"I know, but we can work better with lunch under our belts and a couple of coffees at our sides. We'll pack up, grab a bite at a drive-through restaurant, and head back to Henderson. Once we've made out the letters on the cheeks, if we do, we'll inform the sheriff here and in Virginia of our findings."

I hated to quit when we had just begun, but Renz was right. We could focus on the pictures better if we didn't have to worry about people seeing the images or overhearing our conversation. Reviewing the pictures privately and speaking candidly with each other was the more prudent option.

Once in the car and driving north on our way out of Durham, we grabbed burgers and fries. We ate our late lunch in the car as we headed to our hotel in Henderson.

Chapter 10

With full bellies and two large coffees to go from the hotel's restaurant, we set up our work area in my room only because I had two queen-sized beds. Our supplies were on one while we kept the table clutter-free.

Again, I worked on one side of the table and Renz on the other. We each had paper and pens at the ready and the copied images of our Jane Does in front of us. I went back to my paper that showed the first letter was an *I* or an *L*. Renz did the same with his *O* or *D* then continued. We sat in silence except for the occasional groan of frustration. After a half hour, I had put together what I thought were the letters on Jane's left cheek. I craned my neck to see what Renz had written down. "You done with that side?"

"I don't know. Maybe. What have you got?"

I tipped my head with uncertainty. "Well, I think it reads 'it slit,' but the first two letters are capitalized, so 'IT slit,' which makes no sense at all. And yours?"

"Nearly the same thing, but 'ON slit.' We have to be reading them wrong."

"Maybe my *I* and *T* and your *O* and *N* are initials."

"Then what does 'slit' mean?"

I squeezed my temples. "Hell if I know. Possibly slit like in a knife wound? You know, like, to slit someone's wrists or throat. Where is that magnifying glass when we need one?"

"Enlarge that picture from your phone, save it, and then enlarge the saved image again."

"It's going to get blurry," I said.

"Just try anyway. We may be reading something wrong."

I tapped the gallery with the photos of Jane, found the picture of her left cheek, and enlarged it. I saved it and enlarged it once more until it filled my phone's screen. "Okay, that's about as good as it's going to get."

Renz took the phone and held it under the floor lamp. "Hmm…"

"What?" I crowded next to him and took a look.

"I don't think that first letter is an *I*. Doesn't it look like the cut also goes sideways at the bottom, possibly making it an *L*?"

I squinted. "Yeah, I believe you're right. So LT?"

"Uh-huh."

I let out another frustrated groan. "But what the hell does slit mean, especially on both women?"

"Wait a minute." Renz reached for the phone again and gave that word a long, hard look. "What if it actually reads 'slut'?"

"Come on." I nearly laughed until I realized that Renz was dead serious. "Really? No way."

"Writing small letters like that and trying to keep them legible might cause the fingers to cramp. There's the chance that some letters are deeper or more defined than others. The killer might be giving us a hint."

"But why?" I paced the room as I tried to make sense of Renz's theory. "I doubt that the killer actually wanted the bodies found."

"But if by chance they were found and identified and somebody deciphered the letters, like we possibly did, it would humiliate the victim and their family if somebody was calling those women sluts. Maybe they stepped out on him, one as a first wife and one as a second," Renz said.

"No. They have different last-name initials." I waved my hands in the air. "We're getting ahead of ourselves. Let's just say the letters read LT slut and ON slut, with a slight chance that the *L* is actually an *I* and the *O* is a *D*."

Renz wrote down the different options. "Now we have to decipher the right cheeks."

I sighed. "I could use a stiff drink and an aspirin right now."

"Me, too, but we're on duty, and we're trying to stay clearheaded. We'll get to that after supper and after we've made sense of the letters on the right cheeks."

We knuckled down and got to work. Renz continued with the facial letters, and I logged on to the missing persons database for Virginia. Suspecting both women of being from the state, I would search for women who fit the height and weight of both Janes and who had the initials we'd found carved into their faces.

At three thirty, we took a break to update Taft. Renz said he would call her while I went down to the restaurant and bought two more coffees. We had made progress with the right cheek cuts, and once we compared the updated photos from Forensics, we decided the letters on the women's right cheeks were the same. Renz was going to call Taft and suggest emailing the images and our assessments to see if our FBI forensic lab agreed with what we'd come up with.

I returned to the room just as he ended the call. I passed him a coffee and sat at the table. "So, what did Taft think?"

"I already forwarded the images to her along with our thoughts. She said she'd get back to us as soon as possible with whatever Forensics concluded. It could be tomorrow when that happens, though. I told her you were looking through the missing persons database for Virginia. If you find close potential matches, we're supposed to let her know, and she'll get those missing women on the news outlets. Somehow, some way, those victims will be identified."

"Okay, then I better get back at it. How far back should I look, Renz?"

He rubbed his chin, clearly thinking. "Set it for a month. If we have to push it back again, we will."

I gave him a nod. "We should let Sheriff Crane know what we're doing."

"Yep, and I'll do that now. By six o'clock, we're going to call it a night, though, hopefully with positive results."

With my coffee as a pick-me-up, I resumed searching the database, but there was only so much I could enter as parameters since we didn't have names to go by. I looked and looked again as I felt my eyelids getting heavier. Only fifteen minutes had passed before I pushed back my chair and stood.

Renz gave me a glance. "What's up?"

"Just need to wake up a bit. The coffee hasn't helped."

"Have you found any possibilities yet?"

"Only one so far, but during the last year, there have been plenty of women reported missing throughout the state."

"But that doesn't mean foul play was involved. People disappear sometimes because they want to."

"I know." I sat back down.

"Tell me about the missing woman you've flagged."

"Sure. I flagged her because of her initials, age, height, and weight. I used hair color, too, as a secondary ID since the hair of our victims wasn't tested to see if it's their natural color or dyed."

"And that's something I think should be done."

"I agree," I said. "Anyway, the age, height, and weight fit the range from the medical examiners, so she's a maybe."

"What's her name, and where is she from?"

"Linda Isaac, and she went missing from Richmond. The initials aren't LT, but we did think the cuts could have read IT."

"Right, but no matter the initials, she couldn't have floated to the Woodworth area from Richmond. Somebody moved the victims from the area where they live to where they were dumped in the water. The problem is we know where Virginia Jane was found, near Green Hill, but we don't know where North Carolina Jane went into the water."

"I'll keep looking. We have an hour before you wanted to call it a night. Doubt if my eyes could last beyond that anyway. Got anything on the right cheeks?"

"Yeah, I do. Both women have the same letters spelled out. They read DMMD."

"That's odd, and why the mirror image of the letters?"

"Don't know. Everything so far is a mystery and one that'll likely be tough to solve."

"Well, with both women wearing those same letters, it has to mean something significant."

"Yep, and we'll figure it out, Jade. I promise."

I continued scrolling through the names of missing women. The names meant nothing, and neither did the photos. So far, we were only guessing that the letters etched into the victims' faces were initials, but my search would include those possibilities anyway.

By six o'clock, I'd found four more women with initials matching those we'd written down. I checked the weights and heights before I spent too much time on them. Actually, those were the constants that couldn't change. One woman was too tall and another too heavy, but the remaining two had my full attention.

Deena Norman was from Danville, Virginia, yet the body we were investigating was found sixty miles north of there in a small stream outside Green Hill. I had to keep in mind that not all killers disposed of bodies a block from their home. In fact, to make it harder on law enforcement to find out who the victim was and where they were from, dumping a body a good distance from their home was a smart thing for a killer to do. There was a chance that Deena could be one of the victims. I reminded myself and jotted down that the Virginia victim had pierced ears, too, according to Dr. Finch. I highlighted Deena's information and copied it into a blank document then continued on to the other woman's information. She also had a name that could fit the possible initials—Olive Nells, who went missing from Cave Spring, only fifteen minutes south of Roanoke. She also fit the parameters I'd set, and being close to Roanoke meant she could be the woman who was dumped into the Roanoke River. After she was murdered, she could have been thrown in anywhere along its course before it reached the yard of Mr. and Mrs. Greenley, especially since the river had flooded its banks after the hurricane.

"You done yet?" Renz asked. "I'm ready for supper and that stiff drink you mentioned hours ago."

"Yeah, that's enough for today. My eyes feel like I poured sand into them."

Renz wrinkled his nose. "Ouch, that's a painful analogy."

I smiled and tipped my head toward the door. "Go on. Beat it. Give me ten minutes to freshen up and brush my teeth. I'll bang on your door in a few."

"Sounds good." Renz lifted his arm and sniffed, which made me gag. He chuckled. "Guess I'll freshen up too."

Swapping out tops was a good idea. I gave my armpits a thorough spray of deodorant, brushed my teeth, finger picked my hair, and put on a clean top. I was ready for supper and that drink I'd been thinking about for hours. After grabbing my purse, phone, and key, I stepped out into the hallway and rapped on Renz's door. As he opened it and waved me in, I noticed his phone pinned to his ear. It sounded like he was having a serious conversation with someone, and he was jotting down notes as they spoke. I sat on the edge of the bed and waited, assuming he was talking to Taft. That was quickly confirmed when he said "Good night, Boss" then hung up and groaned.

"What's going on?"

"A fast-food restaurant employee took out the trash last night before closing and found a body in the dumpster."

I knew Taft wouldn't have contacted us unless that body had something to do with the case we were working. I grimaced. "And?"

"And the woman had injuries identical to those of our other Janes."

"Shit. Where was she found?"

"Taft said in Lynchburg."

"And now what?"

"She's going to send the information to your email address. We'll take a look at it after supper. There's nothing we can do right now anyway, and we have to eat."

"Yeah, I'm good with that."

We left Renz's room and headed downstairs. We needed food, beverages, and a mental break from work talk. Afterward, we would take a half hour to read the email to see what the gist of it was and to get the names and contact phone numbers for law enforcement personnel in Lynchburg. We would touch base with them in the morning then discuss the findings with Sheriff Crane. I was sure that at some point tomorrow, we'd move on to Roanoke then possibly Lynchburg too.

I was famished, and if I was, that meant Renz was nearly

comatose. The hostess seated us by the window that faced the main street of town and brought over two waters.

"Can I get you drinks while you go over the menu?"

I smiled. "Absolutely. I'll have a single-malt Scotch, neat, please."

Renz nodded. "Same for me."

"Sure thing, and the sheet just inside your menus lists tonight's specials."

"Thank you." I let out a deep sigh and was about to open my mouth when Renz wagged his finger at me.

"We're on downtime, so appreciate and enjoy it. We don't get it often."

He was right, so I turned the conversation to sports. Renz loved football as much as I did, and we talked about the upcoming games and the parties he would definitely be invited to.

Our drinks came, then we ordered our meals, both of us going with the beef stroganoff special, which included soup, salad, and crusty rolls.

I took a sniff then a sip of my Scotch. I held it in my mouth for a few seconds, wanting the taste to linger before swallowing, and it was delicious.

We spent the next ten minutes reminiscing about some of the football parties from last year. I reminded Renz of the time he'd slept on my couch because he was too inebriated to drive back to Milwaukee.

Those were the times I looked forward to—a busy day of work then a relaxing night of anything *but* work. Good company, good food, and good drinks always made a long day worthwhile.

Our food came, and we dug in. Every course was delicious, and after we finished, we had dessert and coffee. We still had some work to check into, but by nine o'clock, we would be doing our own thing in our own rooms. I planned to shower, wash my hair, and watch a little news before crawling into bed, calling home, and discussing my day with Amber and Kate then drifting off to sleep.

Chapter 11

The TV was nothing more than background noise until breaking news interrupted the program. Chris's head snapped that way. It appeared that the woman in the fast-food restaurant's dumpster had already been found.

"Damn it. Why are the bodies always found within days? Why not months, or better yet, how about never? And Susan was found by a ten-dollar-an-hour dishwasher? What the hell?"

Chris thought back on Susan, the woman hated even more than the others. She deserved every ounce of pain she'd gotten. Every scream and every cry for mercy had gone unheard, and every tear had gone unnoticed. Susan had to pay, and she'd paid with her life, just like the others before her and the last two after her, who would die soon. Susan was an arrogant snob who thought she was better, richer, and smarter than everyone else.

Guess I showed her. Killing her was a pleasure, and I'd do it over and over again if I could. Dissolving that tranquilizer in her water bottle when she went to the bathroom at the gym was all it took. By the time she got home, she was putty in my hands. Cutting her up while she was still alive was the best feeling I've ever had.

Chris laughed. "I watched as the blood drained from her body, then I cut her up some more."

Only a day had passed since Chris had heaved what remained of Susan into that dumpster.

The summer heat must have sped up the decomposition. She had to be stinking in that hot metal can with the sun beating down on it. There's no other way they would have discovered her since she was in that heavy-duty garbage bag. I thought for sure she'd end up in a landfill where she belonged with all the other trash.

After opening the refrigerator door, Chris grabbed a beer and popped the tab.

I have to come up with something else, at least for Ruth. It doesn't take a rocket scientist to figure out that three women with identical injuries probably died at the hand of the same killer. Maybe I'll pour muriatic acid over her face. If it can remove rust from concrete, it can destroy her face easily too. And the last kill will be the best—the crème de la crème.

Chris grinned. "That one will take a lot of planning, and hopefully, death won't come quickly. I want it to take a long time and be agonizing."

Chris thought about the different locations where the bodies had been found. Luckily, none of those locations gave any indication of the killer's home base, and it would stay that way. The women were unknown, each one's home town was also an unknown, and figuring out who had done the killing would be tough even for the best law enforcement officers.

"Good luck with that. I just might get my happy ending after all."

Chapter 12

Downstairs, as we waited to be seated in the restaurant, Renz texted Sheriff Crane. We had new information about the Jane Does to discuss with him along with the latest discovery in Lynchburg.

His reply text said he and his deputies would be interested to hear whatever we had to share, and they could sit down with us at nine o'clock in the morning, again in their cafeteria.

We followed the hostess to our table. Minutes later, a carafe of coffee was dropped off, and the waitress took our order. I waited until she was out of earshot before talking.

"Renz, it's looking like Virginia is our point of origin for the three murders. I think it's time we move on and station ourselves in Roanoke. I also think Jane number one needs to go with us."

Renz tapped his spoon against the coffee cup's saucer. I could almost see his wheels turning. "Yeah, you're right. We need the bodies in one location, and since they all likely originated from Virginia anyway, that's probably where their families are too."

"I'm sure we can arrange it with the sheriff. Jane ended

up here, but that doesn't mean any crime was committed on North Carolina soil. They really don't need to keep her in their custody."

"I agree." Renz paused our discussion with a quick head tip—the waitress was bringing our breakfast to the table.

"Anything else I can get you folks?"

I smiled. "I think we're all set. Thanks."

When she walked away, Renz continued. "I'll suggest that to Taft before we meet up with the sheriff. There's really nothing more they need to do here. The only crime scene, if you will, was the Greenley's yard, and if there was a spec of evidence there to begin with, it washed away a week ago."

"Sounds good to me. So after the meeting with Crane, we'll pack it up and head north?"

Renz stirred a packet of sugar into his coffee. "Yep, that's exactly what we'll do."

I stared. "Since when do you use sugar?"

He chuckled. "Just seeing if I like it."

I rolled my eyes. "Okay, so once we're in Roanoke and settled, I want to track down the next of kin for Deena Norman, who went missing from Danville, Linda Isaac from Richmond, and Olive Nells, who was from Cave Spring. Then, while you drive, I'll continue the search with my laptop to see if I can pin down any more names."

Renz tipped his head toward my plate. "Eat now. Talk later. Your food is going to get cold."

I shook my head. "Yes, Mom."

After our filling breakfast, we headed to the car, where Renz made the call to Taft.

"Hey, Boss, anything more on the body found in Lynchburg?"

"Only that it's in the hospital's morgue right now and the police have been searching the dumpster and immediate area for evidence. They've already interviewed the employee, who really didn't have much to say except for reporting a sickening odor. He told his manager, who then checked out the dumpster and called the police. She said she saw a suspicious-looking black contractor's bag that seemed out of place there in the trash."

"Got it. We're going to wrap up here with the sheriff then head to Roanoke. There's no point in sticking around this area, especially when it seems that the victims were all from Virginia or at least were killed there."

"Yeah, okay, but I want you to view the body in Lynchburg first. Talk to the people in charge at the hospital then learn what you can from the police captain. Roanoke is where the nearest medical examiner is located anyway, so I'll arrange for Jane number three's body to be moved there as soon as possible. Roanoke will be your base until you come home."

"Understood, and we're going to need the Jane Doe that's here moved to Roanoke as well."

"I'll arrange that too. Not a problem."

"What about TV coverage?"

"See the woman in Lynchburg first, report back to me, then we'll get that set up. I'll text you the contact names and addresses."

"Roger that," Renz said. "Jade found a few women from the Virginia missing persons database that we're going to check out. We'll keep you posted."

"Good enough. Talk later."

Renz ended the call and pocketed his phone then pointed the nose of our rental toward town. We would discuss what we had, promise to keep the sheriff updated, and because no crime had been committed in North Carolina, tell him it was time to focus on Virginia. We'd also tell him of the latest discovery in Lynchburg, which was another reason we needed to head north. After our meeting with Crane and his deputies, we planned to return to the hotel, pack our belongings, and check out. The drive to Lynchburg would take two and a half hours if we made a pit stop in between, and as Renz drove, I was hopeful about finding more missing women who matched our victims.

We were a few minutes early to the sheriff's office, which was fine with me. The sooner we left Henderson, the sooner I could get back to my search of missing women from Virginia.

We checked in with the deputy behind the glass wall, went ahead to the lunchroom, and saw two deputies at the table, talking among themselves while they sipped coffee. We joined them and made small talk while we waited for Crane and the other deputies to show up. It looked like we weren't going to get an early start after all.

Minutes later, Sheriff Crane and the last deputies entered and took their seats. Renz got to the matter at hand pretty quickly. He hit all his talking points, explained why it was necessary to move on to Virginia, and said that as far as the FBI was concerned, the case in North Carolina was closed. Renz promised to keep Crane abreast of the outcome and said we appreciated the help that the Henderson Sheriff's Office and Dr. Leto had given us.

With a few back-and-forth questions and answers, we stood, shook hands, and were off. The meeting took less than a half hour.

Once we packed and checked out, Renz programmed the GPS for Lynchburg, made the calls to the contacts Taft had texted him, and told them we were on our way. We wanted to meet with the police captain, review the statements from the restaurant personnel, then stop at the hospital's morgue to see Jane Doe number three. After topping off the gas tank we headed out.

With my laptop and notepad ready to go, I logged back on to the Virginia missing persons database and continued where I'd left off last night. We'd been given a brief description of the latest victim—black hair, five foot four, and one hundred and nineteen pounds. She was similar in size to the two Janes before her.

"I'm getting the feeling that the perp has a certain type of woman in mind to kill."

"Because they're all close in height and weight?"

"Uh-huh. Maybe he once had a wife or girlfriend who resembled those ladies."

"Or a mother he hated who did."

"It could be that too. We can't tell if they looked like one another, for obvious reasons, but Jane one and Jane two had blue eyes, and Jane three had brown."

Renz turned his head. "Did you ever ask about the hair color, dyed or natural?"

"I did but haven't heard back on that, but as we know, Jane one is a blonde, Jane two is a brunette—"

"And Jane three has black hair?"

"That's right."

Renz grunted his acknowledgment then tipped his head my way. "I'll let you get back at it. Mind if I turn on the radio if I keep it low?"

I smiled. "Nope. Go right ahead."

I dug in again with the same parameters I'd set yesterday when I began the search. I wouldn't have to change anything for our latest victim since I wasn't using hair or eye color in my search. I would focus only on height and weight and narrow it down after that.

Occasionally, I looked up and took in our surroundings, read road signs, and stretched. I needed that break from the computer and a gulp of bottled water before refocusing on the task at hand.

"How many maybes do you have?"

"Since I started forty minutes ago, I've added three more."

Renz raised his brows. "That's three we didn't know about before."

I acknowledged his comment then got back to it. I gave the search another hour, then Renz turned off the highway and into a gas station at Brookneal. I welcomed the break.

"I need to stretch, get a coffee, and use the facilities."

"Me too."

We walked into the building together and parted at the restrooms. Once finished, we browsed the snack aisle, grabbed coffees, and waited in line to pay. Renz said he needed to fill up again before we continued on.

"Did Tory book us a room in Lynchburg, or are we moving on to Roanoke later?"

"I think we're continuing on to Roanoke unless we hit a snag. It's just over an hour from Lynchburg."

"Sounds good." I noticed a bonus-sized Snickers on the candy shelf and grabbed two of them.

Renz chuckled. "Are you going to eat both of those?"

"Of course. Why?"

"Then I'll grab my own. You've got me hooked on them too."

We paid for our snacks and coffee, Renz topped off the tank, and we hit the road again in under ten minutes.

So far, I had seven possibilities for missing persons, and they were from all corners of Virginia. I wasn't sure how to work out the logistics, but we would discuss that later. For now, I still had two pages of possible missing women to look through and just under an hour left to do it.

Chapter 13

We finally passed the Lynchburg city limits sign a little before one o'clock. We needed to notify the officials we intended to meet with that we had arrived and see when they could get together with us. If they were at lunch, we would grab a bite, too, and get down to business after that.

Renz pulled into a city park and killed the engine in the shade of a large oak tree. Then he fished his phone out of his pocket and checked the names and numbers again. "I'll call Captain Reynolds to see what he suggests as far as meeting him or the hospital doctor first."

I powered down my laptop and packed it and my notes into my briefcase. I wouldn't need them again until we were seated with the police captain and whoever else planned to join us.

Renz talked for a few minutes then hung up.

"Well, what's the word?" I asked.

"Sounds like he wants us to meet with the hospital doctor first. There's a pretty serious domestic situation going on right now that the police are involved in. Husband has his wife locked in the house with him and is threatening to kill her and then himself."

"Geez, what the hell is this world coming to?"

"You really want me to answer that?"

I swiped the air. "No, it was a rhetorical question. So, we need to contact the doctor, then. What's his name?"

"Hang on." Renz went back to his phone and looked. "Dr. Stanley Adorsell. I'll call him now to see if he can meet with us."

While Renz made the call, I stared out the window at the kids playing in the park. He asked for the doctor, but it didn't sound like he was being transferred.

"Sure, just have him call me as soon as he's done."

I listened as Renz rattled off his cell number, hung up, and looked my way. "You want to go have a late lunch?"

"What's going on with the doctor?"

"He's in the middle of their monthly staff meeting. The person I spoke with said he should be available in an hour or so."

I pulled out my phone to see where the hospital was and find some decent restaurants in the area. "Feel like Mexican, Chinese, pizza, or American fare?"

"Let's do Mexican."

"Okay, that sounds good to me."

I entered the address into my phone and let it guide us to the restaurant. Once we were inside, I saw the typical Mexican décor, which I liked, then we were seated by a host wearing a T-shirt with the restaurant's logo on it. We thanked him, and within a few seconds, a bowl of tortilla chips and two bowls of salsa—one mild and one hot—were delivered to our table. We both ordered nonalcoholic margaritas while we browsed the menu and munched on chips.

I frowned as a thought came to mind. "Hey, did Taft mention the photos you sent her?"

"Of the women's cheeks that Forensics was going to weigh in on?"

"Yeah, those."

"Humph. She hasn't. I'll text her and ask. I'm sure it slipped her mind to mention it."

"That's a big slip, don't you think? I mean, this is an FBI case too."

Renz lifted his phone and tapped the keys. "We'll find out in a minute. Everyone forgets now and then, Jade, especially when their head is filled with numerous cases."

As Renz texted, I realized that I should be a little more patient and forgiving. Everyone was overwhelmed with tasks on occasion, and chances were our forensic team couldn't decipher the letters any better than Renz and I had. I kept quiet and sipped my margarita.

With his phone sitting on the table in case an incoming text came in, Renz picked up the menu again and read through his choices.

"See anything that interests you?" he asked.

"Oh yeah, I'm having the pork tamale platter with rice and beans."

"Hmm… that sounds good. I think I'll have the same except with chicken."

Minutes later, the waitress stopped and took our order then refilled our basket of tortilla chips.

Renz's eyes darted toward his phone. "Looks like Taft just texted me back." He picked it up, tapped the text icon, and read the message. "I guess Forensics was supposed to contact us directly. Taft is getting ahold of them." Renz smiled. "No worries. I guess Forensics has been busy with the cases at home."

The waitress brought out our food, and I paused my thoughts on everything but the meal in front of me. It looked and smelled delicious. As we began our lunch and enjoyed a second margarita, Renz's phone vibrated.

"Looks like a local call is coming in. It's got to be from the doctor's office. I'll be right back."

I glanced around the restaurant, which was still full of patrons even though it was pushing two o'clock. I agreed that Renz should take the call outside, where it couldn't be overheard by people enjoying their meal. While I waited for his return, I continued eating. No sense in letting my food get cold.

He returned within minutes. "Chow down. Dr. Adorsell is expecting us at two thirty."

"I'm almost done. It's you who needs to chow down." There weren't any churros in my immediate future, but I still had my Snickers to enjoy if a chocolate craving hit. Right now, talking to the doctor and seeing Jane number three was far more important.

While Renz shoveled down his tamales, I took care of the check so we could scoot out the door as soon as he was done. Luckily, the hospital was only a mile away according to my phone's map, but we would have to check in, ask for the doctor, and be directed to the lower level's morgue.

We found the hospital easily—it was the largest building in the area. Along the main road, plenty of bright-blue signs with arrows directed drivers to its location. Renz parked, and we walked into the main entrance of the multistory redbrick building.

At the counter, we introduced ourselves and said we had a two thirty appointment with Dr. Adorsell. We got the typical response—sit in the waiting area until someone came to escort us down to his office.

I hoped we wouldn't go through the long wait like at most hospitals, and surprisingly, we didn't. Within five minutes, a volunteer arrived and walked us to the bank of elevators. We rode to the basement level and walked two hallways, then a sign had an arrow pointing down the last hallway to the morgue. The volunteer escorted us through the door, and beyond a wall of glass, a man was sitting behind a desk.

"That's Dr. Adorsell."

"Thank you, and I think we've got it from here," Renz said.

Renz didn't need to knock. The doctor saw us, stood, and rounded his desk to greet us. Renz made the introductions and asked for an explanation of how and when the body had arrived at the morgue.

Dr. Adorsell invited us into his office to talk before we took a look at Jane. That was as good a time as any to pull out my notepad and take a few notes.

"We do intend to speak with the police and the caller who found Jane, but can you tell us the process up to the point where she was delivered to the morgue?"

"Of course, Agent DeLeon. Standard procedure was in place, I'd assume—police, EMTs taking the body into their custody and then delivering her to the hospital. We don't have a county coroner—there's only four cities in the state where they have them—and Roanoke is the nearest one to Lynchburg. Under criminal circumstances, she would have to be taken to one of those facilities, possibly for an autopsy and tox screening if warranted."

"Sure. So bringing her here is kind of like a temporary placeholder."

"That's exactly right. If she died accidentally or under normal circumstances, then she'd remain here until burial or cremation unless the family wanted an autopsy."

"Got it. Do you have the time Jane was delivered to the hospital?"

"I do. It's mandatory to document that information. Give me just a minute to pull that up on my computer. Of course, that was long after I was home, but we have people who take care of that regardless of the time. I checked on her myself when I came in yesterday morning." The doctor rattled his fingertips against the desk as he browsed the hospital documents. "Here we go. Jane was brought in and taken down to the morgue at one fourteen a.m. yesterday."

"So Tuesday morning an hour after midnight?"

"That's correct, Agent Monroe."

I wrote that down. "Without a medical examiner looking at her yet, is there a way to tell how long she's been dead?"

"Roughly, yes, but none of that is exact science. We all know the signs of rigor. Normally, the body temperature is checked, too, but since we don't have a coroner staffed or on call, she was placed in cold storage, so the body temp is a moot point. My best guess was that Jane died sometime Monday. The police have the report of when she was discovered, and because she was at the bottom of the dumpster, I'd assume she was placed inside the can before the restaurant opened that morning. Nobody could dispose of a body during the open hours without being seen, especially since the dumpsters are near the drive-through area."

"Sounds like you know that restaurant well," I said.

"I do," he said. "I worked there myself as a teenager."

I looked at Renz. "Shall we view the body? We'll get more information from the police report later."

"Sure. If you're ready, Doctor?"

"Of course." Dr. Adorsell stood and walked to the door. "Right this way."

We followed the doctor into the refrigerated morgue, where he pulled out drawer number nine. He unzipped the body bag as far as Jane's sternum since what we were interested in seeing was mostly her face anyway.

Before we got too involved with her facial cuts, I asked about identifying features anywhere on her body.

Dr. Adorsell shook his head. "No tattoos and no scars large enough to be noted in a missing persons report."

"Any jewelry on her person?"

"Nothing. She was nude."

"Literally? As in naked and no phone, wallet, or purse found in the dumpster?"

"Nothing that was documented on our end, but the police would have that paperwork."

Renz asked the doctor if he had a magnifying glass.

"Certainly. You're interested in her facial cuts?"

"Yes. We believe among the cuts are letters, maybe even initials."

"Humph. I didn't look that closely, but the slash across her neck is what killed her. She probably bled out quickly." He shook his head as if to erase the images.

"What is it, Dr. Adorsell?" I asked.

"There was so much blood and so many cuts. Because of the volume of blood, I believe most of the cuts were made while she was still alive."

I grimaced at the thought of somebody being that evil, that uncaring, and that dismissive of another human being's life.

Renz held the magnifying glass within an inch of Jane's left cheek. He looked up and nodded. "I see letters or numbers, maybe. It looks like a five and an *M*. After that is the same letters the other women had carved into their cheeks."

"Maybe it's an *S*, not a five."

"I bet it is." Renz walked around the body and looked at her right cheek. He nodded again. "Same thing, DMMD."

I let out a long groan. "Okay, at least we know it's the same killer. It's like he wants us to connect him to each of the women because he's carving the same thing on each of their right cheeks." I snapped off a few close-up pictures of Jane's face.

Renz spoke up. "How soon can this body be moved to Roanoke? We'll be there later today and would like to compare the three bodies side by side tomorrow morning."

"I can arrange for a driver to take her today."

"That would be great. Thank you so much for your time, Dr. Adorsell," I said as I pocketed my notepad.

We shook his hand and left. As we crossed the parking lot, Renz dialed the police station again. We were told the captain was back and could meet with us for a half hour. It was all the time he had. If necessary, we would make copies of the police reports and review them later. For now, we just needed to hear the details, ask a few questions, then leave to talk to the fast-food restaurant employees. Their names and contact information would be in the police report.

Chapter 14

It was three o'clock by the time we were seated on the guest chairs across from Captain Reynolds' desk. We knew he had a press conference coming up about the hostage situation involving the husband who had threatened to kill his wife and himself.

The captain appeared fidgety and rightfully so. I was sure his adrenaline level was off the charts. We were thankful he had time for a short meeting with us.

"First, I have to apologize for seeming rushed. I realize you've been working this murder case for several days now and traveled from North Carolina to meet with me. I'll give you all the time I can spare."

"Understood, so maybe we should cut to the chase. First, we'll need copies of all police reports and statements."

"Not a problem. Everything is still right here on my desk."

"Great. So what did your officers or first responders see when they arrived at the scene?" Renz asked.

"First responders arrived and were shown where the dumpster in question was. Officer Lacy said the odor of death was unmistakable. Unfortunately, he had to climb into the dumpster and confirm that it wasn't a dead dog or some other type of animal."

"That had to be awful," I said. I knew full well the kinds of horrific tasks the police had to perform.

Reynolds sighed. "Agreed, yet more awful for the victim. Anyway, the deceased was a woman, so they got the EMTs out there to remove the body and take her to the hospital's morgue. The police searched the dumpster for evidence of any kind and found nothing other than what one would find in any fast-food restaurant's garbage."

"So how is a crime scene handled when you don't have a forensic team here?"

"We look for possible evidence, bag it if found, and send it to Roanoke. Everything else is based on witness statements. We don't have many homicides in Lynchburg, especially when the victim and suspect are unknowns."

"Got it. Are there cameras at that restaurant?" Renz asked.

"Not outside, but if there were, they wouldn't be facing the dumpsters."

"Good point," I said.

Renz stood. "I guess that's all we need other than copies of the reports."

"Sure thing." Captain Reynolds fed the sheets of paper into the printer and pressed the copy button.

"So, how did that domestic situation turn out?" Renz asked.

Reynolds shook his head. "They're both dead."

I groaned. "That's a real shame."

I slipped the police reports into the side pocket of my briefcase, and we headed out. Once in the car, I took a look at the witness statements and the names attached to them.

"The male employee is nineteen-year-old Matt Stevenson, and the manager on duty that night was Elizabeth Pence."

Renz turned over the ignition. "Okay, let's check out the restaurant first to see if either of them are there, and if not, we'll go to their homes."

"Sounds good. Let me pull up the restaurant location." I searched my phone for Day N' Night Drive-In. "Ah, here we go. Looks like it's two miles from here." I set my phone to call out the directions from the police station, and we were off.

I checked the time that we arrived at the restaurant—three forty-five. A typical night shift crew at most retail locations would already be working, but I had no idea if employees in a fast-food restaurant rotated days or shifts. Renz parked, and we walked in.

I looked around for somebody other than the two girls taking orders at the counter—possibly a person clearing tables. All we needed was an employee to get the manager on duty to come talk to us, and I didn't want to wait in line for that. It didn't look promising.

Renz, much more patient than myself, walked to the line and stood with his hands in his pockets. I gave him my best scowl, pulled out my FBI ID, walked to the side of the counter, and held it in front of the nearest cashier's face. It worked.

"Can you get the manager for me, please?" I asked quietly.

"Yes, ma'am, right away." The cashier disappeared for only a second then returned to her position.

The side door opened, and a frowning woman approached me. "Are you the FBI woman?"

"Yes. Are you Elizabeth Pence?"

"I am."

"Great, then we need to have a word with you and Matt Stevenson."

"Matt isn't scheduled to work today."

"Okay, can we find a quiet place to talk, then? We'll track down Matt on our own."

Elizabeth scanned the restaurant then pointed. "Over there should be good."

We followed her, and when we reached the booth, I made the introductions. "Elizabeth, I'm Senior Special Agent Jade Monroe, and this is my partner, Senior Special Agent Lorenzo DeLeon. We're here about the body found in your dumpster late Monday night."

Her eyes welled up, but she held it together. "Why is the FBI involved? The police are searching for the killer, aren't they? Please tell me that the people of Lynchburg don't have to worry about a killer being loose in our city."

"Ma'am, the police are doing the best they can, but without eyewitnesses or the victim's identity, it'll be tough to make an arrest. We're here to help out since the FBI has far more resources than a local police department does."

She seemed to accept my answer. I wasn't about to tell her that the victim found in their dumpster wasn't the only woman murdered at the killer's hand. There were at least two more that we were certain of.

"Now, can you walk us through what happened that night? We still intend to speak with Matt, but sometimes during highly anxious moments, people exaggerate what they saw, or they forget to include important information." I smiled. "Especially teenagers."

"I understand. Actually, Matt was only involved for a few minutes. We were closing for the night, thank God, so that meant the public doors were locked and we were doing the end-of-the-shift cleaning. There were four of us here. I settled the daily financials, got the tills ready for the next day, and ordered supplies online while the employees filled the containers, mopped, cleaned all the surfaces and restrooms, and took out the trash. As the manager, I have to stay until everyone has clocked out, then I set the alarm and lock up."

"Do you know what time Matt took out the trash or when he came in to get you?"

Elizabeth sighed. "Yes, it's ingrained in my mind. I always keep a mental note of important things."

"That's good to know," Renz said.

"We close at eleven, and our after-hours work takes approximately an hour. Matt had six bags of trash to take out, and he had them lined up at the back door. It was on his first trip out to the dumpster that he informed me of the smell. That was at eleven fifty. I grabbed a second flashlight and went out there with him. The rancid odor hit me a few feet before I even reached the dumpster. I knew that wasn't normal."

"So you suspected something was very wrong?"

"Absolutely. Our dumpsters never reek like that. I didn't want to, but since I was the manager on duty, I had to look in. That's when the flashlight's beam landed on a black contractor's bag at the bottom of the dumpster. Just the length and shape of it told me it wasn't a bag of trash. I rushed in with Matt, told him to lock the back door, then dialed 911. As soon as the police arrived, I sent everyone except Matt home. The police wanted to speak with both of us. I told them exactly what I told you, and Matt's story was the same."

"Okay, then what happened?"

"Then I called our regional office and asked what I should do. The cleaning wasn't done, but everything was put on hold. They said to do whatever the police instructed."

"Which was?" I asked.

"Lock up and leave."

"So both of you left and didn't see what took place after the police told you to go home."

"That's correct. The regional office said to have the morning shift come in an hour early and finish what we didn't before they open for the day but only if the police let us. I called them first thing Tuesday morning, and they said it was okay to resume regular business hours."

"Has the restaurant had any problems with vagrants lingering around, dumpster divers looking for food, or any looters in the area? Anyone being a problem inside the building?"

"No, not at all. Everything has been totally normal, and I've worked here for eight years as a manager and three years before that as a cashier."

"Okay, I think that's all we need except for Matt's phone number. It wasn't listed in the police report."

Elizabeth dipped her hand into her back pocket and pulled out her phone. "Sure thing. I have it right here."

Renz programmed the number into his phone, then we thanked Elizabeth for her time and left. Before driving to Matt's home, where he lived with his family, Renz tried Matt's phone. There wasn't any sense in driving to his house if he wasn't there. His family couldn't answer our questions on his behalf.

Luckily, Matt answered. Renz spoke for less than a minute, thanked him, and hung up.

"Is he home?"

"Yep, let's go. I'd still like to get to Roanoke before dark."

In less than ten minutes, we made it to the Stevenson residence, where Matt, or at least a young man looking his age, sat on the porch and watched as we drove up and parked. Renz and I got out and approached him.

"Matt?" Renz asked.

"Yeah, that's me."

I noticed that he wiped his hands on his pants before shaking ours. Sweat caused by anxiety, I imagined. His hand was clammy and cold when I shook it. The poor kid was afraid.

"You want to talk inside or out here?"

"Can we talk out here? My mom gets really upset when I mention what I found. She insisted I quit my job, but I'm nineteen and can work where I want."

I smiled and thought about teenagers. It was crazy that I'd

actually been one once. "We can talk wherever you want."

"How about the backyard? We have a picnic table in the shade."

"Sure," Renz said. "Just lead the way."

We reached the backyard and took seats facing Matt. He looked shaky.

"Matt, there's nothing to worry about. We've already spoken with your manager, Elizabeth, so we have most of the timeline and how the discovery happened. We just need to hear what you remember," I said. "Take a deep breath, calm your nerves, and start whenever you're ready."

"Um, okay. I didn't actually see the bag, Elizabeth did, but it was the smell that made me go inside to get her."

"Right, and death has a strong odor that's hard to forget. So you were taking out the trash?" I asked.

"Yeah, I just began. I already smelled something foul when I got close, but I had to lift the lid to toss in the bags. That's when I dropped them and ran back inside. I knew something bad had happened. Elizabeth came out with me, and the smell was even worse."

"Because the lid was open?"

"I guess so. She shined the flashlight inside, swore a little, and rushed me back into the building. That's when she called the cops."

Renz took over. "And what happened when they got there?"

"Two cops talked to Elizabeth and me, and a whole bunch of them were outside. We were there for about a half hour, and then the cops said to lock up and leave. I noticed the EMTs had already arrived by then."

"Have you worked since?"

"I did yesterday, but somebody else took out the trash. The other night manager, Tom, said from now on, there has to be two of us that go out to the dumpsters when it's the end of the night."

"A good idea," I said. "I think that's it, but if anything else comes to mind, you can call me. Here's my card."

He pocketed the card and walked us to the front of the house.

"Thanks, Matt, and stay safe."

As we walked to the car, I glanced over my shoulder and saw Matt step up to the porch. He looked at us and waved. I waved back, then he entered the house and closed the door.

"Time to head to Roanoke?" I asked as I opened the passenger-side door.

Renz nodded. "Yep, but how about you drive while I rubberneck and take in the scenery?"

I grinned. "Sure. I can do that."

Chapter 15

We arrived in Roanoke at five fifteen and checked into the hotel Tory had booked for us. After freshening up, we left to find the police department. We wanted to meet the chief face-to-face before morning then set up a plan for tomorrow. We also needed to know if the other two bodies had arrived from Lynchburg and Durham.

Renz's phone rang just as he parked. It was our forensic team back in Milwaukee with their take on the cuts on the cheeks of Jane one and Jane two. Renz set his phone to Speaker so I could weigh in on the conversation too.

"Hey, Agent DeLeon. It's Hal from Forensics."

"Tell me something good, buddy."

"Well, between the four of us, we concur. We believe the cuts are initials, and on Jane one, we agree that it reads LT and then 'slut.'"

Renz elbowed me across the console.

"And Jane two?"

"We're in agreement that it's a D and an N. The right cheek on both is a DMMD."

"And we thought that too. I'm going to have Jade send

over a few pictures of Jane three. Same markings on her cheeks. If those markings are actually initials, it could help us find out who the women are."

"Sure thing, sir. We'll get right on that. My apologies for the mix-up. I guess I didn't hear the part about us sending you our findings."

"No sweat. Text me after you guys come up with those last initials. I'll have Jade send the pics over now."

"Roger that."

Our short-term plan was to meet with the chief in charge of the city police department, Dan Taylor. There was also a county police department similar to a county sheriff's office, but since the body was discovered within the city limits, they weren't involved.

We walked in and told the officer behind the counter that we were there to speak with Chief Taylor. Luckily, the chief came out quickly and greeted us then said he looked forward to talking. Since he had been kept abreast of what time we would show up, he said he had already checked on the arrival of the bodies at the medical examiner's office—they were both there.

That was a relief and one less thing for us to worry about. It also meant that first thing in the morning, we would gather with the chief, the officers who had been on scene, and the detectives to go over everything we knew.

We joined the chief in his well-appointed office and sat facing him. We would keep the conversation to a minimum since we were going to discuss the case with all of them tomorrow.

"For now, a brief update will do. I don't want you to repeat everything a second time in the morning."

Renz nodded. "We were thinking the same thing. What we need from you is to have everyone here in the morning who had something to do with the discovery and whoever will be working the case going forward. We believe all the women are from this general area give or take fifty miles in any direction. We also believe the killer is one and the same for the victims because of the way the faces are carved. We'll explain that in detail tomorrow."

"But there aren't any suspects at this point, correct?"

"That's correct, sir," I said. "We don't even have names for the victims yet, but that might change by tomorrow."

"Good to know. So there is a chance of solving these heinous murders?"

"Absolutely," Renz said. "So what time and where should we meet in the morning?"

"We have a second-floor conference room that I think we can all fit in. Let's make it ten a.m. That'll give you time to speak with the coroner, compare bodies side by side, and get his take on it. As far as I know, he's making the comparisons right now."

"And by morning, we should have more information from our own forensic experts back in Milwaukee," Renz said. "We intend to speak with our supervisory special agent after we leave here and air the information we've learned about these women on the news throughout Virginia."

"That should get people talking."

"And that's what we're hoping for." I stood. "We should

let you update your officers, and we need to set something up with the medical examiner for the morning." I extended my hand and shook his, and Renz did the same. "We'll talk more tomorrow at ten o'clock."

After leaving the building, Renz made the call to the coroner, Dr. Raymond Morgan, set up a time to see the women in the morning, and hung up. The last work-related call we needed to make for the night was to Taft. We had to update her on Jane number three and let her know Forensics agreed that the cheek carvings consisted of letters that were possibly the first and last initials of the victims.

"That's a significant discovery," Taft said as I listened in on the call. "As soon as Forensics looks at the latest photos Jade sent and comes up with initials for the last victim, I want you to go back to the Virginia missing persons database and only look for women who have those initials. If we're on the right track, their height and weight should match what the coroners' reports show too. If they do, we'll put that information on the news while we try to find relatives who can confirm without a doubt that our Jane Does are their missing loved ones."

I sighed. "That still doesn't give us the killer."

"I know, Jade, but the initials on the right cheek were the same for all three, correct?"

"That is true," Renz said.

"Then maybe they're the killer's initials."

I frowned at Renz and shook my head. "Why would a killer squeal himself out?"

Taft chuckled. "Jade, what are the top common traits of serial killers?"

"Self-indulged, narcissistic, they think they're smarter and better than most, etcetera, etcetera."

"Exactly, and that means they assume they'll never be caught. I doubt that this killer realizes we've noticed the cuts are initials."

"Maybe he thought the bodies would never be found," Renz said.

"Maybe, but why carve any initials at all, then? I believe the killer is taunting us, or he wants the victims exposed for what he thinks they were—sluts."

Renz let out a groan. "This is a tough case, that's for sure."

Taft chuckled. "True, but if we figure out who the women are, it'll move along quickly. There's something or someone all three women have in common, and we'll figure it out. For now, you're off the clock. Have supper, get some rest, and check back in once you hear from Forensics. We'll get those initials on the news along with what we have of the victims' descriptions. Good night, Agents."

"Good night, Boss."

Chapter 16

The hardware store's automated doors opened, and Chris walked out with a jug of muriatic acid in hand. It was time to put it to good use, and Ruth was the next name on the list. After Ruth, there was one more person to kill, then Chris would be finished. It would be over, and everyone responsible for Chris's predicament would be dead—as they should be.

Ruth's demise had been given deep thought. For simplicity's sake, the murder had to be done in her own home, and as long as Chris came and went unseen, it wouldn't matter. Nobody would know who killed those women or why, and the cops weren't smart enough to figure it out.

Although, leaving her at home in an acid-filled bathtub might make it too easy to identify her. Maybe I should dump her somewhere after all. I won't make it easy on the detectives because that's what they get paid to do—detect. They need to work their tails off to figure out who I am.

Chris checked the time. Ruth wouldn't be home for another half hour. There was just enough time to sneak inside and lie in wait. That night, Ruth would get her personalized beauty treatment—an acid facial to die for.

After checking the exterior of Ruth's house and making a trial run yesterday, Chris knew the neighbors wouldn't give a delivery person an ounce of attention, especially at suppertime. Ruth had a screened front porch too—a plus in Chris's eyes—and that black screen would help keep anyone inside nearly invisible. A lock-picking tool was all it would take to get into the house and wait for Ruth to come home, where she would be in for the surprise of her life.

Chris headed directly to Ruth's house, an easy seven-minute drive from the store in Roanoke. The empty box used for the fake flower delivery now held the jug of acid. A tan ball cap sat on the passenger seat next to it. The props looked legit. After parking around the corner, Chris walked the short distance to the home on Rose Drive then let out an involuntary chuckle. In fifteen minutes, things would become far less rosy for Ruth.

A quick look up and down the street told Chris the coast was clear. It took only a second to get past the screen door to the porch. Now, kneeling to unlock the house door, Chris was invisible to anyone looking out their window or walking by. Several attempts with the lock-picking tool was all it took. Chris was in and quietly closed the door. The house was small, so finding a good place to hide wouldn't take but a minute.

Do I wait and let her settle in or blitz her as soon as she walks through the door?

Chris weighed the odds. Right away and the fun would

be over with too soon. Ruth might even scream before the front door was closed. Waiting and watching would be much more exciting.

Since it was an eighty-degree day, Ruth wouldn't be hanging a coat in the closet when she walked in. Most women didn't hang a purse in a closet either.

Her purse will likely be placed on the kitchen counter. I'll hide in the closet and leave it cracked just a little so I can watch her, at least in the living room and part of the kitchen.

Chris opened the closet, stepped in, then pulled the door within a half inch of closing. Seeing Ruth milling about would be entertaining until Chris grew bored.

That's when I'll strike her with this jug of acid, knock her senseless, and drag her ass into the bathroom. When she's lying in the tub, I'll pour the acid all over her but mostly her face.

After getting comfortable in the closet, Chris waited but not for long. The hum of the overhead garage door opening said that Ruth had arrived, and the fun was about to begin.

Chris heard the door open from the garage into the kitchen, then shoes clip-clopped against the tile floor. Looking through the narrow space, Chris saw a woman's hand drop the purse on the breakfast bar then disappear into the kitchen. The refrigerator opened, a bottle rattled, and the refrigerator closed. Next came the hiss of the bottle cap being removed. Chris grinned.

Who wouldn't pop a beer when they got home after a long workday? Poor Ruthie. Your time to enjoy that beer is short. Make the most of it, kick back, and relish your last hour alive.

Seconds later, Ruth appeared from the kitchen and took

a seat on the couch facing the TV. She grabbed the remote and began channel surfing.

Chris could see her only from the shoulders up since the couch was in front of the closet, but it would be easy to sneak up behind her and club her in the head with the jug.

Hmm… but will she see my reflection in the TV screen? Maybe that blitz attack will be a better idea when the time is right.

Chris wasn't one to sit around and do nothing. Ruth might watch a movie, remaining motionless for hours unless she got up to grab another beer. Or she might turn off the TV and make a meal instead. Chris waited to see what Ruth was going to do before jumping into action.

If she goes into the kitchen, I'll sneak out of the closet and take her by surprise when she walks into the living room. Yeah, that'll work.

It didn't take long. Ruth paused the reality show she'd been watching and walked down the hallway. Chris heard a door close, likely the bathroom.

It was time. Chris quietly stepped out of the closet and took up a position just outside the bathroom door. Surprise was everything, and the second Ruth opened the door, it would be lights out for her. Being right there at the bathroom anyway was a plus in Chris's eyes—no need to drag Ruth far.

The toilet flushed, then came the sound of water running—Ruth was washing her hands. Chris stepped back against the wall and watched the door handle. Soon it would turn, the lights in the bathroom would go off, and Ruth would step out.

A second later, Ruth was in the hallway and turned left. Just as fast, Chris raised the jug and bashed Ruth's head with it, causing her to stumble and fall forward. Twice more, Chris slammed her in the head with the heavy jug. Groaning, Ruth tried to get up, but Chris kicked her in the back, knocking her to the ground again.

"You're done, bitch." Chris grabbed Ruth by the leg, dragged her into the bathroom, and rolled her over the edge of the tub, where she hit the bottom with a *thud*. "Time for your acid bath. Maybe Drew can help you again. Oh, that's right. There's no point since you'll be dead."

Ruth's head flopped to the side. She was nearly unconscious, but Chris wanted her alert enough to feel the acid eating away at her skin. Chris turned the cap and opened the jug.

Slapping Ruth across the face, Chris yelled, "Hey, snap out of it!" Ruth looked up, and they locked eyes. "Hold it right there. Don't move a muscle. That's perfect." Chris poured the acid over Ruth's face and watched as the liquid bubbled, sizzled, and ran down her throat. Ruth screamed and flailed, but nobody heard her cries for help. Chris ripped open Ruth's blouse and continued to pour but made sure her face had been completely saturated before moving down her body. "I've heard adding vinegar helps dissolve soft tissue. Don't go anywhere. I'll be right back." Chris headed into the kitchen and saw the pantry.

If you have any vinegar, it would be in there.

Chris opened the louvered door and spotted a bottle of vinegar on the second shelf. "Perfect."

Back in the bathroom, Chris poured the vinegar over

Ruth then continued with the acid. It wasn't long before the jug was empty.

"I should have bought two. Oh, well."

Chris pushed up the window, walked out of the toxic-smelling room, and went to see what looked tasty in the refrigerator. Ruth, or what was left of her, would be disposed of later.

Chapter 17

After supper and several glasses of wine, I told Renz I was going to hit the hay early. I wanted to get a leg up on investigating those initials. There was more research to be done on the woman with the initials DN that I'd found yesterday in the database. A Deena Norman from Danville had gone missing over a week ago and hadn't been heard from since. That timeline fit with Jane Doe number two, who was found along the stream near Green Hill. She could actually be Deena Norman.

What I wanted to do was shower, sit in bed with my laptop, and learn more about Deena. I sighed and looked at the clock. As much as I wanted to call the person on record who had reported her missing, I hadn't been given the go-ahead, and I needed a second set of eyes on Deena's description before making a move like that anyway. Making that call could either give the family some closure or it could be a devastating setback for them if I was wrong about Jane Doe number two being Deena. I would search for more people online who might be related to her. Her mother, who lived in Baltimore, had reported her missing, but it would be helpful if I could find a family member who lived closer. I also needed to go through the database one more time to see if any new names had been entered that could match our dumpster victim and the LT who was confirmed with Forensics as the Jane Doe found on the Greenley property.

After parting ways with Renz, I showered, washed my hair, and put on my pajamas. On the bed, I propped pillows behind my back and opened my laptop.

Okay, the report said Deena lives in Danville. Let's see if the internet can tell me something about her.

I had no idea what Deena did for a living or if she was some public figure whose name would pop up on an internet search. For all I knew, she could be the typical next-door neighbor who had never done a single thing that warranted public attention, but I typed her name into the search bar and waited. That name came up in California and Minnesota, neither of them a state I was looking for, and the ages weren't right either. I narrowed my search to Deena Norman, Danville, Virginia. The only thing that came up was a link to the police station's missing persons database, which gave me an idea. In the morning, I would call the Danville Police Department and ask if anyone besides the mother had called or stopped in about Deena going missing. That could lead me to other relatives or neighbors who might know more about Deena or point to someone who did. If none of that helped, we could go for the phone records, which could take months to get, but if Jane number two wasn't Deena, then our time would be wasted while waiting for information on the wrong person. There had to be a way to learn definitively if that unnamed woman was Deena.

I jotted down a reminder of the things I needed to do tomorrow besides what was already scheduled. We also had to find out if the women's hair color was natural or not. According to the missing persons report for Deena, she had brown hair, blue eyes, and pierced ears—all traits that matched Jane Doe number two. There was hope, and I planned to discuss that hope over breakfast with Renz.

At the moment, though, I needed sleep and felt the two glasses of wine kicking in. After my nightly call home and some much-needed shut-eye, if luck was on our side, tomorrow we would learn something after comparing the bodies. Then with Taft taking the reins on the case, we'd get the victims' descriptions aired on the news stations throughout Virginia.

The last thing I remembered after saying good night to Amber was closing my eyes—and then I heard my phone's alarm go off.

It was hard to believe morning had come. I had slept so soundly that my eight hours of sleep seemed like eight minutes. I was awake, refreshed, and ready to kick Thursday off to a productive start.

I tapped out a text to Renz saying I would bang on his door at seven thirty. Since we weren't meeting the police chief until ten o'clock, that gave us plenty of time to have breakfast and pay the medical examiner an in-person visit.

After a quick rinse, I dressed, drank two cups of coffee, and checked my emails. I went over my to-do list, which included talking to Forensics about the initials on our third Jane's face. With the confirmation of initials on all three

Janes, we could air that information on the news and still do our best to match up the LT and the initials on our last woman with the missing persons database, especially if new reports had come in.

I was sure Deena was one of our unidentified women, but I needed to convince Taft and Renz before going out on a limb and contacting her mother.

After brushing my teeth and combing my hair, I gathered everything I needed for the day, placed it all in my briefcase, and left the room. I took two steps across the hall and knocked. I knew Renz would be ready to go, and he was. He grabbed his room key, pocketed that and his phone, and we were off.

The restaurant wasn't in our hotel, but it was next door in a standalone building—not a big deal in my eyes unless it was raining, and it wasn't.

As we drank coffee and waited for our breakfast, I went over my research with Renz. I was seventy-five percent certain that Deena Norman was Jane number two.

He listened to my reasoning as I discussed the similarities between the women, then he took his turn.

"So we don't have any identifiable features to use as proof, and there aren't any prints for a Deena Norman on record, you said."

I nodded. "No, there aren't."

"Then how do we prove it's her?"

"Maybe through blood typing. She was brought here right after she was discovered, and I'm sure Dr. Morgan took a blood sample, if for no other reason than to rule out the chance that Jane was drugged before she was murdered."

"That could work if Deena's mother knows her daughter's blood type."

"Even if she doesn't, it could be on record somewhere like at a hospital or a doctor's office. Or maybe she donated blood in the past."

"All good ways to find out, but you know what that means, right?"

"Yes, we'd have to contact her mother. How about we meet up with Dr. Morgan, ask if he drew blood from Jane, and if he did, find out the type. We'll compare bodies like we were going to anyway, and if there's time before we meet with the police chief, we'll call Taft and see if she'll give us the green light to go ahead."

We finally had a plan of action, at least for one of the victims. If we were able to learn more about Jane one and Jane three and had a lot of luck, we would find the nexus that connected all of them, and that nexus would be the killer.

We ate our breakfast silently, no doubt with plenty of thoughts and ideas running through each of our heads. By eight thirty, we were in the car and headed to the medical examiner's office on Northside High School Road. Late yesterday, Renz had confirmed an eight forty-five appointment with him via email.

We arrived a few minutes early, entered the building, and after showing our IDs, asked for Dr. Morgan. We were told we could take the elevator to the lower level, where his office was located. After we spent a few seconds in the elevator, the doors parted and we exited one floor down. I immediately saw the sign that read Medical Examiner's Office, yet I wasn't surprised to learn his was the only office on the bottom floor. That was where nearly every ME's office—as well as a hospital's morgue—was located.

We walked into a small room, where a woman sat behind a desk. I assumed she was the doctor's secretary. We introduced ourselves and said we had an eight forty-five appointment with the doctor. She raised her index finger and said she would let him know we were there. After a quick call to the room on the other side of the wall, she said he would be right out—and he was.

It literally took five seconds before his door opened and he welcomed us in. I appreciated his promptness.

We sat facing his desk to get a few questions and answers out of the way before we viewed the bodies. My first question was about the blood.

"Was blood drawn from Jane Doe after she was here and in your custody?"

"Yes, I take samples from each body I deal with. You never know if it might be needed at some point. I try to cover every possibility."

"And did you test it for anything?"

"No, since it was obvious how she'd died. Even if the killer drugged her first, the manner of death was the same—a slash across her neck, just like the other two."

"So by seeing all three bodies, you concluded that the manner of death was identical?" Renz asked.

"I most definitely did. Actually, other than the hair and eye color being different, and maybe an inch taller or shorter and five pounds heavier or lighter, those three women were very similar. None of them had identifying marks on their bodies, and of course you know that they were all sliced up badly."

"Doctor, to get back to Jane's blood type, what was it?" I asked.

"She's type O."

"Okay, we're hoping we can confirm who she is by her blood type. She might be a woman I found in the Virginia missing persons database."

"That would be wonderful if you could give her a name, but keep in mind, type O is the most common blood type."

Renz sighed. "We'd like to give them all names. Speaking of the women, can we have a look at them now?"

"Certainly."

Dr. Morgan rounded his desk and escorted us to the morgue, where we saw three drawers pulled out, the women lying side by side and the body bags fully unzipped with a sheet covering each woman from the neck down. It was a sad sight, especially because those women were blank slates. We knew nothing about any of them, and their families didn't know where they were. Until they were positively identified, if that happened, the county would bury them as Jane Does with a small grave marker to show their final resting places. It wasn't right, and I would do my best to give each of those women a name and a proper burial with their loved ones attending.

Renz and I stood between the drawers, at the end where the women's heads lay. With the bodies side by side, it was easy to see how similar the vertical slashes were.

"Doctor, would you say the perp is left- or right-handed?"

"Definitely right-handed, and that's because of the throat wound. It goes from left to right." The doctor rubbed his chin. "No matter what, there is one thing I can tell you about the killer."

Renz's eyebrows shot up. "And what is that?"

"The killer hated each of these women and deliberately wanted to destroy their faces."

"But that was just to keep them from being identified," I said.

"I'm not so sure. There are far easier and quicker ways to do that. Drop a heavy boulder on their face, take a sledgehammer to it, and so on."

I flinched. "So then why?"

"It's like every slice made the killer happy. They wanted to prolong the destruction because they enjoyed doing it. I don't believe these women were random victims. I think even if the killer didn't know them personally, maybe they knew of them. Maybe the women did something that angered the assailant."

That comment brought me back to the word "slut." Had the killer targeted women he thought were loose, immoral, or destined for hell because they carried on with multiple men? Did he kill because of religious beliefs? Dr. Morgan's comments had opened a whole new thought process for me and possibly a reason the killer had murdered those women. Did the women think too much of themselves, were they too pretty, or were they a magnet for men—possibly married men? I groaned as I thought about that possibility. Now we had a new motive to look into.

Chapter 18

We thanked Dr. Morgan and made our way to the police station. With a little time to spare, I wanted to make some of the phone calls on my list before we went inside.

My first call was to our Milwaukee-based forensic team since we hadn't gotten confirmation yet about the women's hair color or what the team came up with as far as initials for Jane number three.

Leah Jasper answered the phone on the second ring. "Forensics, Leah speaking."

"Hey, Leah, it's Jade."

"Hi, Agent Monroe. I know why you're calling, and I was just about to reach out. We have the information you're looking for whenever you're ready."

"I'm ready, so go ahead."

"Okay. Each woman's hair color is natural—blond, brown, and black."

"That's great and makes everything easier. And the initials?"

"We came up with SM."

"Good, so did we. That's all I needed. Thanks, Leah."

"You bet."

I hung up and noted on my list what she had said. "So, should we call Taft and tell her what we know so she can arrange the news coverage?"

"Let's organize the descriptions, locations where the victims were found and when, along with the initials for each woman before we email it to Taft. I'm sure she would appreciate some form of organization," Renz said.

"Sure, but we should call her and let her know."

"Yep, we will. We also need to tell Taft about the possibility of Jane number two being Deena Norman and our thoughts about comparing their blood types. Meaning, do we contact Deena's mother or not?"

"Taft will have to make that decision, so we may as well call her now. We still have ten minutes before our meeting starts."

Renz made the call while I listened in on Speaker. He told our boss everything that we had discussed over breakfast, then I added the part about contacting Deena's mother.

"The blood type won't give us an absolute answer, Jade, but DNA will. Call the mom, have her overnight some of her own hair strands to Roanoke. Make sure she knows that the follicles have to be attached. Get Deena's blood type from her, too, in some type of official document. It has to be on record somewhere. Get the address for Roanoke's crime lab and have it sent there. The medical examiner can pull DNA from Jane, and we'll have it compared. That's the only way we're going to be able to identify her. If we find names that correspond with the initials for the other two victims, we'll go through the same process. So, when can I expect to get the email from you?" Taft asked.

"As soon as the meeting is over with the police chief and his people, I'll put something together and send it to you."

"Okay, that sounds good. I'll let you know when you can expect to see something on the news."

With that, we said goodbye and entered the police department. The meeting was about to begin. Surprisingly, a man who introduced himself as Chief Taylor stood in the lobby, awaiting our arrival. We didn't even have to ask for him. We followed him to their briefing room, where three officers and two detectives joined us. The chief made the introductions, and we all took our seats. During the next half hour, Renz and I explained our plans, the similarities between the women, and Dr. Morgan's thoughts about the case when we'd spoken to him earlier. We asked for names of sketchy people who might be capable of killing. We also asked about criminals who had recently been released from prison and returned to their hometown and possibly their old ways.

"Don't get me wrong, Agents. We had sixteen murders last year, up from the year before. Each and every one of those killers is locked up and doing life behind bars. We don't go easy on criminal activity in our town."

"Good to know. Any gossip around town of a religious nutcase who wants to make sure everyone is living a godly life come hell or high water?" I asked.

Chief Taylor looked at his staff. "Anything like that ring a bell?"

They muttered among themselves then said no.

The chief continued. "The biggest obstacle I've seen is that we don't know the women, can't identify them, and have no idea where they're from or why some unknown person wants to kill them."

I sighed. "And the fact that they're dumped in other parts of the state doesn't help. Hopefully, if we can get a positive ID on the Jane Doe who was found in the stream at Green Hill, it might lead to a domino effect where each woman is connected to the other through the killer. We should know something tomorrow, and when we do, Chief, you and your staff will be the first to know. Also, later today, the descriptions of each woman will be aired throughout the state on the major cities' local news. With any luck, that'll help. What we need is a dedicated eight hundred number for viewers to call here at the police station and, of course, people to man the phones."

Taylor nodded. "I'll get on that this afternoon."

We thanked the chief and his crew then left to get those descriptions and initials put together to email Taft. The sooner the citizens of Virginia were made aware of the three Jane Does, the sooner we would catch the killer.

We sat in a small coffee shop across the street from our hotel. I had my laptop with me to compose an email to Taft. After ordering two coffees, Renz and I dug in and began with everything we knew about Jane number one. After that, we did the same with Janes two and three. Each woman's information included where she was found, how long she'd been dead, cause of death, height, weight, hair and eye color, and approximate age. We included the initials, but that was for Taft's information only. We didn't want the killer to know we had deciphered the initials. We had yet to figure out what the DMMD stood for. I assumed it was more initials, DM, but the mirror image was a mystery to me.

The email was sent off, and it would be a while before we knew when to expect the news in Roanoke to air the broadcast. That was the only broadcast we would see, but I expected it to be the same across all the news stations in the state.

"There. That's taken care of."

"Now—"

"I know. Now we have to call Deena Norman's mother in Baltimore." I smiled at Renz. "You wanna do it?"

"Not on your life. Women communicate better with women and men with men. Go ahead. You've made tough calls before. Besides that, we don't actually know that Jane and Deena are one and the same, but any parent would do whatever they needed to do in order to know the truth."

My groan was my response, so I packed up my briefcase, reached for my phone and the notepad I'd written the mother's information on, and walked outside. Earlier, I'd seen a bench in the shade, and that was where I would make the call. The mother, Rita, was a fifty-five-year-old widow, and there was a good chance she'd just lost her only daughter. I dreaded the second she answered, but giving bad news was part of my job, and I had to suck it up and get it done.

I waited as the phone rang on Rita's end. I didn't have the words rehearsed or written down. I would talk from my heart and hope she realized that the only way to know whether Jane was or wasn't Deena was to follow my instructions.

"Hello."

"Hello, ma'am. Are you Rita Norman?"

"I am. Who's this?"

"My name is Jade Monroe, and I'm an FBI agent in the Serial Crimes Unit. I'm in Roanoke, Virginia, right now, and I'm investigating the deaths of three unidentified women."

I heard what sounded like crying. "Yes. And?"

"And I came across Deena's description in the Virginia missing persons database. Ma'am, we have no way to know if one of our deceased women is Deena without knowing her blood type and getting a DNA sample from you so we can see if it matches our woman in question."

"But her photograph was with the report."

"I understand that, and the description of Deena closely matches our Jane Doe. She has natural brown hair, the height and weight matched along with the eye color, and Deena had pierced ears, right?"

"Yes. So why can't you compare her photograph?"

I grimaced. "Ma'am, the victim's face has been damaged." That was the easiest way to say we couldn't physically identify her without going into detail. "With your help, we could tell you if she is or isn't Deena. What we'd need is a few strands of your hair with the follicles intact overnighted to the crime lab here in Roanoke. They'll compare your DNA to the victim's to see if there is a familial match. Also, do you know Deena's blood type?"

"Yes, it's the same as mine, type O."

"And is that documented somewhere?"

"It's noted in her file at the doctor's office."

"Great. Now, Mrs. Norman, are you willing to find out if this unknown woman is Deena?"

She began to sob. "Of course I am. I was thinking of moving to Virginia to be close to Deena, but then she went missing. I've been sitting on pins and needles since hoping that she'd be located but not like this."

"And you have my deepest sympathy either way, but this truly is the only way to find out. If you can overnight those hair samples right away, we'd appreciate it. Please send a copy of the blood type too. I have the address whenever you're ready."

"All right. Go ahead."

Chapter 19

After hanging up, I gave Renz a sad look. "I guess we wait until tomorrow. With any luck, we may be able to ID one of the victims." I shook my head. "But what good does that do without someone to pin the murder on?"

"It does plenty good, Jade, and you know that. If Jane is actually Deena, the mother will be able to bury her daughter and try to deal with her grief, and we may get closer to finding the killer. Like Dr. Morgan said, the killer knew who those women were, and by finding Deena's friends and asking around, we could get lucky."

"There's that word 'lucky' again. None of this was lucky for the victims."

"True, but it's going to be even less lucky for the killer as soon as we find him."

I let out a groan. "I know. So, you want to grab an early lunch? After that, we can go through the database again. Plus, I want to call the Danville Police Department to ask if anyone else reported Deena missing and, if so, who they were. We can get somewhat of a head start, then by tomorrow, we'll know if we should follow through on Deena being Jane two or not."

"Sure. We're in a holding pattern anyway and don't have anything pressing to do after lunch."

After dropping off my briefcase, Renz and I walked to the restaurant next to the hotel. I wasn't super hungry, but if we ate now, we would be able to work until suppertime and get a lot accomplished.

In the restaurant, I ordered a bowl of homemade chicken dumpling soup and a Cobb salad. On the road, I never seemed to eat as healthy as I should, and a bowl of greens would do me good. I ordered a glass of iced tea to go with my meal. Renz ordered a double cheeseburger, waffle fries, and a soda.

A half hour later, we were done and walking to the hotel. The food was great, and we would be back later for supper.

We decided to sit outside near the pool but far enough away that nobody would overhear our conversation. It was a beautiful afternoon, and getting extra vitamin D never hurt anyone. I returned to my room, grabbed my briefcase, and took it outside. Renz had already opened the umbrella enough to keep the glare off my laptop's screen so we could browse the database again.

I set up the parameters and left the search in Renz's capable hands. "Why don't you go ahead and look for women with LT and SM initials but keep in mind their height and weight. I'll call the Danville PD and find out what they know."

With Renz behind the computer and browsing the database, I made the call and asked for a Sergeant Freeman. He was the sergeant in charge of the missing persons unit, and Rita had spoken with him when she reported Deena missing. It was an unusual situation since most people went to the police station in person when they filed a report, but since Rita lived in Baltimore, she had to fill it out over the phone and through emails.

After two transfers, I was speaking with Sergeant Freeman. I introduced myself, told him why I was calling, and said I needed about fifteen minutes of his time. He seemed shocked when I said we had an unidentified Jane Doe in Roanoke who might be Deena Norman.

"I remember speaking with her mother, Nita. No, it was Rita."

"That's correct," I said, "but we don't know definitively if our Jane is Deena, although we should by tomorrow. I've spoken with Rita, and she's going to send her own hair samples to check against our Jane's DNA to see if we get a match. Other than Rita, has anyone come in or called with concern about Deena's disappearance? Maybe a neighbor, a coworker, a best friend, or a boyfriend?"

Freeman went silent for a few seconds. "Well, that was more than a week ago when Rita called. I better check on the computer. I can barely remember yesterday at times."

I chuckled. "Believe me, I know the feeling."

"I did send some officers out to her residence, though, to conduct a wellness check. Nobody was home, none of the doors were ajar, and nothing looked out of place. I'll admit, we haven't been back since. I'd imagine her mailbox would be pretty full by now if she hasn't returned."

"Good point. Did the officers talk to the neighbors?"

"Yep, and nobody knew anything. I can email you a copy of the police report."

"That would be helpful. Thank you."

"Ah, here we go. It doesn't look like anyone—wait a minute. There was a blocked call from a man who said he was concerned about her. He said he normally spoke with her every other day, but he hadn't for quite a few days. She hadn't answered his calls, and her voice mailbox was full."

"That's interesting. What was the guy's name?"

"That's the weird part. He wouldn't say."

"Do you have Deena's phone number on file? I didn't get it from Rita."

"Sure, one second. Ready?"

"Yep."

The sergeant rattled it off, and I repeated it back. "And Deena's address?" He told me, and I wrote that down too. "Depending on if we get a DNA match, there's a chance that my partner and I may be stopping in tomorrow or the next day."

"Absolutely. The FBI is always welcome in Danville."

I hung up and asked Renz how the search was going.

He laughed. "I've only gotten through one page, Jade. Have some patience."

"That's impossible. Are you searching by height and weight or the initials?"

"You're the one who set it up."

"Damn it. Did I forget to hit Save?"

Renz shrugged. "Just set it up again, and we'll look together."

I programmed the parameters one more time, hit Save,

then we looked. "There can't be many missing women with those initials, so it shouldn't take but a few minutes."

I was right, and it didn't take long to find two women with the initials LT. I jotted down their names and the search pages where they were found. We didn't find anything on our latest victim, SM, though. I did a quick search of the women who were just added that day and still came up empty.

"Hmm."

"What?" Renz asked.

"Well, the last victim was found Monday night, meaning she possibly went missing Sunday night or in the early hours of Monday. Today is Thursday. Doesn't that seem like a long time without somebody wondering where she is?"

"Yes, but maybe she doesn't have anyone in the area. It's possible she was going to leave on vacation when she was murdered, and nobody knows anything is wrong. There could be other reasons she hasn't been reported missing, although I can't think of many. Everyone has somebody somewhere, but maybe they only communicate once a week."

"I guess."

We headed into the business center to begin the search for family members of the women with the initials LT. They were Lorraine Tilley and Linda Thompson. I set up my laptop again, pulled up the pages their names were on, and hit Print. There was only one option to choose—the business center's printer—so I tapped that button, and the description for Lorraine Tilley printed. I did the same with Linda Thompson. Since nobody else was in the room, we decided to sit at one of the round tables and conduct our work from there. It also didn't hurt that there was a coffee counter with a large variety of pods only steps away.

I looked at the printed sheets and saw that Lorraine Tilley was from Clarksville, Virginia, and Linda Thompson was from Waynesboro. Either of them might or might not be Jane, and because she was found in North Carolina, we could only guess where she was from. On my laptop, I pulled up a map and compared city locations. Because Deena Norman was from Danville, and Clarksville was much closer to Danville than Waynesboro was, I decided to work on Lorraine Tilley first. I tapped the computer keys and entered Clarksville, Virginia, into the people search database. Only one Tilley was listed, Lorraine herself. That told me she didn't have family in the area, so I needed to conduct a wider search. The person who filled out the missing persons report for Lorraine didn't have the same last name, and when I called, nobody answered that number. I left a message and would try again later. No matter what, I wanted to focus entirely on Lorraine until I found a relative, spoke to them, and asked for the same things we had asked of Rita. After that, I would move on to Linda Thompson and do the same.

I widened my search to the entire state of Virginia, hoping that would be faster than guessing where Lorraine might have relatives. I found four other Tilley's scattered across the state and began calling. I planned to ask only if they were related to a Lorraine Tilley and see if that went anywhere. If it did, I could dig deeper.

I'd spoken with two of the four people so far, and neither

said they knew of a Lorraine Tilley. I was baffled by the fact that someone other than a relative had reported her missing.

Renz interrupted my search by suggesting something I hadn't thought of. He said that Lorraine might have grown up in foster care, and that could be why no relatives were looking for her. I had to admit it was a legitimate suggestion and could very well be true. The thought of not having any relatives—or relatives who were known—saddened me. I couldn't imagine a life that empty. There was also the chance that Tilley was a married last name and she had gone back to her maiden name after a divorce, although that was nothing but speculation. After scratching the first two Tilley's off my list, I called the third name, a Thomas Tilley in Richmond. He didn't know Lorraine either. I was striking out and had only one more number to try in Virginia. After that, and because LT could be the initials of someone in any state, I didn't know how we might find a relative unless the news coverage actually did the trick. A concerning thought crossed my mind.

"Hey, Renz."

"Yeah."

"What good will the news coverage be if I can't even find a relative in Virginia? The broadcasts are only being aired in the larger cities in the state."

He rubbed his chin. "Good question, but since the person who filed the report was from Clarksville, you'd think they'd see the segment on the news."

I persisted. "How often do you watch the news?"

Renz chuckled. "Never on TV. I read it on my phone."

"Right, and Clarksville is two and a half hours from Roanoke. What news stations do they even watch there?"

"I don't know, Jade. Maybe the easiest way is to keep trying to reach the person who reported Lorraine missing."

I groaned my frustration. "I know, but nobody answers."

"I'll work Linda Thompson, and you keep trying Lorraine. You still have one number to call, don't you?"

"Yep, and I'll do that right now."

"I know one thing that usually works," Renz said.

"What's that?"

"To have a positive attitude."

I smiled. "Sorry. I guess I worry too much."

"That's our job as FBI agents. We're supposed to worry. Take a breath, and I'll get started on the names in the Waynesboro area."

Minutes later, Renz's cell phone rang. I looked at him as he glanced at his phone. "It's Taft." He answered on the second ring. "Hey, Boss."

I motioned to him to put it on Speaker so I could listen in. Renz did then centered the phone on the table.

Taft began by saying she had reached the news stations in Richmond, Roanoke, Lynchburg, and several of the large touristy cities on the coast. "Unfortunately, the largest cities are a distance from where the crimes took place. In my opinion, I'd say your best leads will come from the broadcasts in Lynchburg and of course Roanoke. Both are set to air at six o'clock. How are the missing person name searches going?"

I told Taft that we weren't having a lot of luck. "The

easiest way will be to speak with the people who reported the women missing, but to get a positive ID, we'll still need a DNA match, meaning we'll have to find a family member."

"That's correct, Jade. Hopefully by tomorrow, we'll at least know if Jane number two is Deena Norman or not. Maybe we'll get lucky with the news broadcasts."

We thanked Taft for the update, and Renz hung up.

"We should call Chief Taylor and let him know when the broadcasts will air. He needs to have the tip lines ready to go"—I looked at my watch—"in two hours."

Chapter 20

Chris had spent Wednesday night and most of Thursday inside Ruth's house. The bathroom door was closed, and the windows were open, yet the toxic smell of acid and decomposing flesh was nauseating as well as dangerous to breathe. The odor permeated the house.

A towel helped block some of the stench when Chris stepped into the bathroom to take a look. The slut hadn't dissolved as quickly as Chris had hoped. Looking down at the sludge and spongy bone fragments remaining in the tub, Chris wondered how to get Ruth out of there.

Damn it, I should have done better research or dumped her last night before she turned into a pile of goo. I'm not in the mood to deal with this, and I don't have a way to scoop her out of that bathtub anyway.

It was late in the day—suppertime, actually—just like yesterday when Chris arrived and lay in wait to blindside Ruth. Now a decision had to be made—leave Ruth in the tub, where she could be immediately identified, or figure out how to remove her and dump the remains somewhere else.

Chris paced in indecision, trying to figure out the best option.

What is my end goal? I know what I still have to do, but am I willing to go to prison for life, be killed by the cops, or is it my intent to get away scot-free? Can Ruth be connected to anyone else I've killed or to the last one on the list? It would take forever, if the cops are even that good, to make the connection. I'm leaving the bitch right where she is, and I need to get out of here before someone complains about the smell.

Leaving Ruth in the tub meant Chris had to wipe down every surface that had been touched, remove the empty jugs from the home, and lock up as if nobody had ever been there. The best time was at that very moment, when most people were enjoying supper. Chris got busy and made sure to put everything in the box the jug of acid had been placed in yesterday. Nothing would go in Ruth's trash can since that was the first place cops usually looked.

A half hour later, after doing a final walkthrough of each room and pocketing Ruth's phone, Chris took the box, put on the tan ball cap, twisted the lock on the inside knob, and walked out of the front door. The car was still around the corner, and it was time to go. Chris stepped out of the screened porch, looked both ways, then headed down the sidewalk.

Taking Ruth's phone could buy an extra day or so. Luckily, nobody had stopped by or called while Chris was at the house.

"So far, so good, and I'm saving the best for last."

Chapter 21

Renz got lucky when he contacted the Linda Thompson relative who had filed the missing persons report. Unfortunately, she was related only through marriage and couldn't help with a DNA match.

"Are you the wife of her brother?" Renz asked.

"No, I'm the wife of Linda's uncle. We were supposed to get together several days ago, but I can't reach her. I went to her house, and it looks like the mail has been jammed in the box for over a week."

"Doesn't Linda have parents nearby?"

The aunt sighed. "They're estranged. It's a long story, Agent DeLeon."

"Understood. Does Linda work?"

"Yes, at Shop-and-Save right here in Waynesboro."

"Okay, I need to contact them, see what they know, and I'll get back to you. Thank you for your help."

"So, she isn't a direct relative?" I asked when Renz hung up.

"Nope, the wife of an uncle. I don't even know how close the DNA match is between uncle and niece. I need to call Forensics and ask."

"I have that answer. It's about twenty-five percent. I'd say that's still a positive match."

"Then he needs to provide us with a hair sample so we can compare DNA with the Jane who was found in North Carolina." Renz looked at the printout. "I'll call Mrs. Thompson back."

"And I'll tell Dr. Morgan to pull DNA samples for both her and Jane number three." I again tried calling the friend who had filed the report for Lorraine Tilley. Still no answer. Renz suggested I call the Shop-and-Save in Waynesboro to hear what they could tell me about Linda while he called the aunt.

After asking for the manager on duty and telling him who I was, I asked about Linda Thompson, how long she had worked there, and how long she had been absent from work. Terry Phillips, the manager, said she was scheduled to work on Monday, Wednesday, and that day, but hadn't shown up at all. They had called her numerous times until a message said her voicemail was full.

"Did she work last weekend?" I asked.

"She worked Saturday, had Sunday off, then was expected back to work on Monday."

That gave me a timeline of when Linda could have gone missing—either later Saturday or anytime Sunday. I thanked him and hung up. Until we had DNA proof of our Jane Does being the missing women, we couldn't invest all of our time on one in particular. Janes one and two were in a wait-and-see position, and Jane three, our dumpster Jane, hadn't shown up in the database at all.

My mind went back to the DMMD on each woman's cheek. I doodled the initials on my notepad and stared at it. "Wait a minute!"

Renz had just ended the call with Linda's aunt and was promised that the uncle's hair samples would be overnighted to the crime lab in Roanoke. "What?"

"Maybe we're looking at those right-cheek initials all wrong."

"In what way?"

"The left cheeks had the women's initials and the word 'slut.'"

Renz raised a brow. "Right?"

"And maybe the right cheek does too. The first DM could be initials just like on the left cheek, and the second set of letters might hold some kind of meaning."

"But if they're abbreviations, then the letters would have to stand for Doctor of Medicine."

"Exactly. We could have been looking at it all wrong, thinking it was only a mirror image when we should have been searching for a doctor with the initials DM."

Renz jerked his head toward my laptop. "There's no time like the present. We have to wait for the hair samples to arrive tomorrow anyway. Let's see if there are any doctors in Roanoke with those initials."

With a furrowed brow, I asked how we would go about doing that. "We'd have to search every type of medicine, wouldn't we? Is there a listing somewhere that shows every doctor's specialty and their name on one site?"

"Hmm… type in the phrase 'doctors in Roanoke, Virginia' and see what comes up."

I did and found the results wouldn't be too daunting. "Okay, the specialty comes up first, then every doctor is listed after you click on that field of medicine."

"Not a tough task, but we'd need to check the entire state or possibly farther than that."

I tapped my fingernails against the table as I thought about the best and most efficient way to address our predicament. "Well, if we're being logical, we would check the cities that Deena and Linda are from. I'll call the person again who filed the report on Lorraine, but no matter what, we already know she was from Clarksville. That means we should try Clarksville, Danville, Waynesboro, and Lynchburg, where our SM woman was found, before we expand to other cities."

"Yeah, I'm on board with that except we only have one laptop between us." Renz glanced at the row of computers in the business center.

"Fine. I'll go find someone out front and ask if there's a charge to use one of their computers and what the log-in is."

Renz grinned. "Thanks, partner."

I shook my head, let out an overly loud sigh, and left the room. When I returned, Renz was already hard at work looking up doctors' names on my laptop. I took a seat at the computer closest to him, plugged in the log-in information, and got online.

"Okay, what city did you start with?"

"I'm working on Lynchburg. Figured we could get the northern towns out of the way and then start on Clarksville and Danville."

"Sounds good to me. Hey, wait up."

"What?"

"The six o'clock news begins in five minutes. We need to watch that then get back to the search."

Luckily, the business center had a large wall-mounted TV with the remote lying on the shelf just below it. Renz hit the green button, and the TV powered on.

"What are the local news channels?" he asked.

"Hang on." I asked my phone and got the channels, and Renz chose the one that came in best.

With the television only a few feet from where we were working, we remained in our seats and settled in to see the broadcast.

It wasn't covered as a breaking news event, but it was the first news piece after the second segment began. The anchor explained that three deceased women, all likely from Virginia, had recently been found in remote locations. He said they were unidentifiable but probably in their thirties. One had blond hair and blue eyes, one had brown hair and blue eyes, and the last had black hair and brown eyes. All had shoulder-length hair. Each woman was between five foot two and five foot four and weighed approximately one hundred twenty pounds, give or take. None of the women had tattoos, but the brunette had pierced ears. The bodies were located in Green Hill, Virginia, Lynchburg, Virginia, and Woodworth, North Carolina. Foul play was suspected in all three cases. The police departments in Roanoke and Lynchburg were taking tip line calls, the news anchor said, then the numbers came up on the screen.

I let out an unimpressed groan.

"Want to explain that?"

"Well, what the hell, Renz? We'll never get anywhere with that, but I bet the police will be bogged down with calls based on the vague descriptions."

Renz stared at the table. "I know, and giving the public their initials could help dramatically, but Taft thought if the killer knew we had discovered the initials, then he would change his manner of murder, and we wouldn't get any more clues."

"That's if murdering is something he plans to continue," I said. "Let's get back to our doctor search. At least that feels productive to me."

Chapter 22

We were striking out with our search. Lynchburg and Waynesboro provided nothing except a loss of hope. Maybe I was wrong after all. Maybe the letters were just mirror images for a reason only the killer knew.

"Why the gloomy face?" Renz asked. "We still have two more cities to check before we even get to the largest cities."

"I know, and I'll quit being pessimistic. Buck up, Monroe, and get it done."

Renz laughed. "You never know. The next doctor could be the one. You take Danville, and I'll take Woodworth."

With a nod, I knuckled down and got busy. I was about fifteen minutes into my search when I yelled out. "I've got something, Renz! And it isn't what I would have imagined."

"Then spill already."

"There's a cosmetic surgeon named Drew Mills who has a practice in Danville."

Renz frowned. "Do cosmetic surgeons go by MD?"

"Yep, I just checked. They're actual medical doctors and have the same degrees as any other doctor. They continue their education in the cosmetic and plastic surgery field then use that as their specialty."

"Okay, that's interesting. Set him aside until we finish with Danville and Woodworth, then we'll see what he's all about."

By seven thirty, we had completed the doctor search in the cities we were most interested in. Drew Mills was the only doctor of any kind who had those initials.

"Now what do we do?" I asked.

"Well, let's start with a deeper investigation into his practice. Show me where you found him."

Renz grabbed a chair and took a seat next to me. I clicked on the About Me tab, and we read it together. The doctor's bio detailed where he grew up, where he went to college, his field of study and degrees, and it said he opened his practice in 2014 in the heart of Danville. There wasn't any mention of a wife, kids, or hobbies.

"Okay. So far, he sounds like a normal guy," Renz said.

"He has a normal bio that is very generic. It doesn't give us any idea who the man actually is, only his qualifications. We need to see if he has a criminal record."

"Yeah, I see your point. I'll check on your laptop. We can't do a background check on somebody on a public computer."

Now it was my turn to take a seat next to Renz. He opened the website that the FBI used to check backgrounds of suspicious characters and typed in Drew Mills and Virginia as the state. "Drew isn't short for anything, is it?"

I shrugged. "I've never known a Drew, but I don't think so."

He nodded, and we waited. Seconds later, the results popped up—no criminal history. The man was clean, and I wasn't surprised. Maybe he was the killer, and maybe he wasn't, but if he was, then he certainly would take every precaution to avoid being caught.

"But that doesn't make sense."

"What doesn't?" Renz asked.

"If he's really the killer, then why risk putting his initials on the women's faces?"

Renz's eyes lit up. Something was percolating in his mind. "Okay, he's a plastic surgeon and maybe a very narcissistic, self-centered one at that."

I leaned in and waited for the aha moment.

"What if he considers himself an artist? I'm sure most cosmetic surgeons do. You mix conceit with his self-perceived artistic flair and what do you have?"

"I give up. What?"

"You have an artist who signs their work. Maybe he screwed up the victims' faces and they were going to sue him. To avoid that, he destroyed their faces and killed them, but as a vain person, he initialed his work."

"That's a good story but kind of far-fetched."

Renz chuckled. "Is it? Think of all the serial killers over time who have taunted law enforcement to find them. Of course, they think they'll never be caught because they're far smarter than the police or FBI. Sometimes it takes years, but when they are caught, the look of astonishment on their faces is priceless."

"That is true. So do you really think that's what happened?"

Renz sighed. "I'm not sure, but the only way to know more is by digging deeper."

"I don't think we have a case, Renz. Someone else could have cut those initials into the women's faces to set him up. Or maybe the initials are wrong. Or—"

"Or we're on the right track and have to find evidence. We'll never get a warrant for his client list or to search his home or office without substantial evidence. If we're wrong, we could ruin a reputable doctor's practice and life."

"But before we do anything regarding him, we need to know without a doubt that Deena is Jane number two and Linda or Lorraine is Jane number one." I grinned. "If we have that information, we could ask Rita if Deena has ever had cosmetic surgery. We could learn enough about the doctor to justify that warrant."

"Okay, I agree. There isn't much we can do tonight except have supper and call it a day. Tomorrow should prove interesting, though, and I'm looking forward to finding out more."

I rubbed my hands together. "And as they say, the plot thickens."

Chapter 23

Chris turned on the TV. It was Friday morning. Surely by now, last night's news segment about the women should have gotten results. Chris watched and waited, yet nothing was said about the murdered women.

Guess I did a good-enough job on their faces that the rest of the descriptions are too vague to help. The cops will never be able to identify any of them, and they haven't even found Ruth yet. I actually think I'm going to get away with this. One more to go and I'm home free.

Because the final murder would be the most difficult, it had to be planned to perfection. A single mistake, one slight hiccup, and everything could change. Chris would definitely be the one to die if anything went wrong.

At the kitchen table, with one eye on the TV, Chris spent the next several hours plotting the last murder—the coup de grâce. It had been a long road getting to that point, but the time had finally come, and Chris couldn't wait.

Chapter 24

After breakfast, Renz and I worked in the business center while we waited anxiously for the overnighted hair samples to be tested for a DNA match. If neither sample matched our Jane's DNA, then we would have to insist that Taft give the TV stations the information about the initials carved into the cheeks of our victims. We might be forfeiting the ace up our sleeves, but there was a bigger chance that by revealing that information to the public, we might catch the killer sooner.

Over a cup of steaming coffee, I made a call to the police station. We needed to know if they'd had any luck last night with the tip-line calls. I was told that the officers were going through the most promising leads, which would be handed off to the detectives. As of that moment, though, they had only a dozen leads to work with.

Disappointed, Renz and I did more online investigating into Drew Mills while we waited to hear from Forensics. The second it was confirmed that Jane was Rita Norman's daughter—if it was confirmed—I would begin asking Rita more direct questions. For now, we had to bite our tongues since we had nothing that implicated Dr. Mills.

"You know, there is something you can do to learn more about the doctor," Renz said.

"Yeah, what's that?"

"Set up an appointment with him."

"What!"

Renz chuckled. "Just a consultation for a facial peel or something like that."

"Gee, thanks. Don't you think he'd wonder why a woman whose address is in North Bend, Wisconsin, would come to Danville, Virginia, for a facial peel?"

Renz swatted the air. "You're overthinking things. Say you're here for a month visiting your mom. You can at least make the call to see if you can get in for a short consultation. See what the doctor is like up close and personal."

The more Renz talked, the more he made sense, yet I doubted that the doctor did those kinds of procedures. Even if he did, he likely didn't do the consultations. "That's probably something an aesthetician does, not the actual surgeon."

"Still, getting your foot in the door is a good first step."

I grinned. "That was a clever statement."

Renz patted his own shoulder. "I do my best."

"Fine, I'll make the call."

I looked up the clinic's number, called, and before someone answered, Renz quickly told me to set the phone to Speaker. Within two seconds, a woman answered.

"Born Beautiful, Angela speaking. How may I help you?"

"Hello, I'm looking to set up a consultation appointment with Dr. Mills."

"Regarding?"

"Um, a facial peel I guess, or something like that to smooth out my skin."

"So, you're getting fine lines, age spots, and crepey skin?"

"Yeah, all of the above." I flipped Renz the bird.

"Well, Dr. Mills is still at his yearly conference in New York, but if you'd like a consult with an aesthetician, we can arrange that for later today."

"Oh, darn. I thought he was only going to be gone for a few days. There were other procedures I wanted to discuss with him."

"No, sorry. He's been gone for two weeks, so we're excited he's finally coming home. We're booking farther out for him, but the consultations can be done by our nurses or aestheticians."

"Okay, I think I'll wait. When will he be back in the office?"

"On Monday. Would you like an appointment for next week?"

"I'll call back then." I hung up and gave Renz a wide-eyed look. "I can't believe it isn't him. We're barking up the wrong damn tree."

Disappointment was written across Renz's face. "Hopefully, those few leads will give us something to work with." Seconds later, his phone rang. "It's probably Taft wanting an update." Renz fished his phone from his pocket and frowned. "It's Captain Taylor, but you just talked to the police station."

"Maybe one of the leads is legit," I said.

"Maybe." Renz answered, said uh-huh, yeah, and several

curse words likely thrown in for good measure. Then he said we would be right there and hung up.

"What the heck is going on?" I asked as I put everything into my briefcase.

"We need to take over the leads the PD got from the tip-line calls."

"Okay. No big deal, but why the cursing?"

"They have another murder on their hands."

"Shit! Same MO?"

"The details are sketchy. I guess two officers went to conduct a wellness check on a homeowner and smelled a toxic odor coming from the house. They went into the rear yard, where the smell was the strongest, saw a bathroom window open, and realized the odor came from that room. With the chief's okay, they breached the house and found something in the tub."

I frowned. "Something in the tub? You mean *someone*?"

Renz shook his head. "It wasn't exactly clear, but we need to take a look for ourselves. Come on. Let's go."

We arrived at the police station minutes later and asked to speak with the chief. Either we would get a logical explanation then take over the tip-line leads, or we would join the detectives at the home the officers had gone to.

Chief Taylor met with us in his office. The expression on his face showed he was clearly shaken. "I've never heard of such a thing, but according to the officers who conducted the wellness check, there are decomposed remains in the tub but not decomposed naturally."

"Can you explain that better?" Renz asked.

Chief Taylor groaned. "Decomposed likely with acid. A hazmat unit is en route, and I told my guys to wait outside the residence."

"What the hell? Were they able to tell if the body was male or female?"

"No, but the homeowner on record is a female named Ruth Bedford, thirtysomething and single."

"Who called in the wellness check?"

"Her best friend, who has tried to reach her since Wednesday night. Apparently, she called and texted several times yesterday, and finally this morning, after still no response, the friend called us."

"We'll need to speak with that friend. This isn't necessarily an FBI situation and doesn't sound like it's related to our case, yet killing somebody with acid that requires Hazmat to remove the remains isn't normal."

"Not that murder is a normal behavior to begin with," Renz added, "but this sounds especially disturbing. I think we need to take a look before Hazmat removes the body. Besides that, we don't know that the deceased is the homeowner. Maybe Ruth Bedford did the killing."

Renz's words stuck with me. Was it a coincidence or a deliberate act since we now had another murder victim who couldn't be identified?

"Forensics has to process every room inside the home. We need to learn with absolute certainty who the person in the bathtub is. Meanwhile, we're going to need a couple of hazmat suits and the home's address," Renz said.

Chapter 25

It was obvious that we were close to the home on Rose Drive. The street was barricaded at the nearest intersections to through traffic, not that residential streets were overly busy anyway. When Renz pulled up, an officer stood at the barricade nearest us.

"Sorry, sir, you'll have to back up and take another street."

Renz held out his badge and faced the officer.

"FBI? Okay, go ahead."

We waited as the officer moved the barricade out of the street.

He called out as we passed, "Make sure you don't block any of the emergency vehicles."

I wondered what kind of emergency there could be after the fact, but the white hazmat van was there along with two squad cars, and I was sure Forensics would arrive soon. I pointed at an open spot where Renz could parallel park. We would have to walk past only three houses before arriving at the one where all the action was taking place.

Renz flagged down one of the men wearing a white-hooded jumpsuit and a respirator.

For the second time in less than five minutes, Renz pulled out his badge. "We need to get inside before the body is removed. We also need two hazmat suits and respirators to use."

The man lifted the respirator from his face. "One minute, Agent. I have to go inside and get the supervisor in charge."

We waited at the sidewalk for several minutes until that same man stepped out of the house with another man at his side. He pointed at us then went about his business. The other man, the one who I assumed was in charge, headed our way while pulling off his respirator.

He called out as he got closer. "I'm Joe Brand, the lead here. What can I help the FBI with? We've got to clear the fumes out of that house."

Since Joe seemed somewhat bristly, Renz took the lead. "We're in Roanoke investigating several murder cases. We need to see that body before you take it away."

"It isn't a body anymore, and you aren't protected from the toxic odor."

"Then we'll need two respirators to use. Hazmat suits would be nice too." Renz stood his ground until Joe nodded.

"Fine, but time is of the essence. If we don't dispose of that mess soon, we're going to have environmental and air-quality complaints flooding our phone lines."

"Understood. Can a DNA sample be taken from the remains?"

"Not my field." Joe jerked his chin to our left. "Ask them. The respirators and suits are in the back of the van. We can't dillydally around."

"Right."

We looked to our left and saw the forensic guys heading our way. They needed to suit up as well.

Without saying anything else, Joe turned and headed for the house.

As we slipped on the hazmat suits, Renz asked about the DNA. "Will the substance that killed that person destroy their DNA?"

"Possibly, but first, we'd have to know what the toxin was. If the body is already decomposed like we've heard it is, then the chances are that acid was a factor and the DNA may very well be destroyed. We'll have to pull some samples before Hazmat disposes of it."

Renz tipped his head toward the house. "Then let's go have a look."

My head spun with images of what we would find in the tub, none of them good. I didn't vomit easily, but I wasn't sure I had ever seen anything as horrific as what we were supposedly about to see. I would know soon enough whether I was going to lose my breakfast or not.

We walked into the already crowded hallway and past two of the Hazmat workers. After excusing ourselves several times, we reached the bathroom. The forensic team asked that everyone exit for the moment so they could get a few pictures before the entire room was compromised. I was sure it already had been.

Renz and I stood back while Forensics snapped pictures of the fabric from the victim's clothes that remained in the tub. After seeing strands of hair still intact, I elbowed Gavin, the forensic specialist we had spoken with outside, and asked if he could take pictures of and bag some of that hair. He gave me a nod and continued photographing what was in the tub and the rest of the bathroom. He scooted back and allowed Renz and me a look.

There wasn't much that resembled a body. Melted flesh and congealed bone were all that was left of the person. Because the fabric that remained was peach-colored, I assumed we were dealing with a female, and I made note of the blond hair. I left the room and headed into the bedroom, where several framed photographs sat on the dresser. One picture showed two women at Disney World, one a blonde and the other a redhead. I wondered if that was the friend who'd called in the welfare check. We would soon find out.

I returned to the bathroom, tapped Renz's shoulder, and tipped my head toward the bedroom. He followed me, and I showed him the picture. After unfastening the Velcro tabs on my jumpsuit, I reached into my pocket, pulled out my phone, and snapped a picture of that photograph.

"Let's get out of here. I'm sure the PD will have their detectives go through the house, and we can meet up with them later. Right now, we need to find that caller and talk to her."

I pulled Gavin aside and told him I needed copies of everything he and his team had gathered and photographed. I gave him my card and asked him to call later in the day. With that, Renz and I returned the gear to the Hazmat van and left.

Once we were closer to our car, I sucked in a mouthful of

fresh air before speaking. "Do you think it's a coincidence that the remains in the tub are unidentifiable, like the others?"

Renz pulled back, seemingly surprised. "Do you think the cases are related?"

I shrugged. "I have no idea, but we need to learn more about Ruth Bedford and why someone hated her."

"Or why she hated someone else that much."

I huffed. "And once again, that's the problem. We don't know who the hell the victim is."

We headed directly to the home of the caller, and while Renz drove, I checked in at the crime lab with the remaining members of the forensic team, who compared our victim's DNA to Rita Norman's and that of the uncle of Linda Thompson.

After hearing the results, I punched Renz's shoulder. "They have a match. Deena Norman is Jane number two!" I felt elated, but it was a short-lived sense of happiness. All it meant was that our dead Jane now had a name and that Rita could bury her daughter and have closure. It was a victory for us but a time of sorrow for the survivors, and learning the victim's identity still didn't lead us to a suspect.

After calling first to make sure she was there, we neared the home of Ruth's best friend. So far, we had the identity of only one victim, and that discovery had confirmed that the initials on the women's cheeks were actual clues. As soon as we caught our breath, we would continue down that path, but first, we needed to know if the remains in the tub belonged to Ruth Bedford. We hoped to find out plenty about her from the best friend, Dani Simpson.

Renz pulled along the curb in front of Dani's house minutes later, and we headed to the door. It took only one knock before she opened it. I held my badge toward her so she wouldn't have to ask who we were, and I immediately noticed the red hair.

"Agents, please come in. We can talk in the living room."

I didn't know if anyone had contacted her after the wellness check, but I was sure she'd figured out that something bad must have happened or the FBI wouldn't have been knocking on her door.

Dani pointed at the couch, and we sat down. She faced us on the love seat and stared as if waiting to hear the words most people dreaded.

"Is Ruth dead?"

Not really knowing how to respond, I looked at Renz and let him take the lead.

"We aren't sure, Dani."

"How can you be unsure? She's either alive or dead. There's no in-between." Tears rolled down her cheeks as she waited for an explanation.

I pulled out my phone and showed her the picture I had taken at Ruth's house. "Is this Ruth?"

Dani looked at the photograph. "Of course it is, and that picture sat on her dresser. You were at her house, so why can't you say what's going on? I'm worried sick about her."

"There are human remains in the home, but we can't confirm that they're Ruth's."

The stunned look on Dani's face spoke for her. She needed to understand what I meant by that.

"Dani, the remains can't be identified," I said.

"Are they burned?"

Renz spoke up. "No, but we can't go into detail. What we need from you are answers to anything that will explain what happened to Ruth, if the remains are even hers. I will say that we are leaning that way since you haven't spoken to her since Wednesday evening."

"And I texted her a million times since then without getting a response."

"Dani, what does Ruth do for a living?"

"She's a paralegal at a law firm downtown."

"Do you know if anyone would want to harm her, and if so, who that person might be?"

"Not at all. Ruth has a great life, and she recently hinted around about a man she was seeing."

"Really? What did she say about him?"

"Only that they were getting closer every day, that he was very attractive and a professional. I assumed he was an attorney at the firm. Ruth was kind of secretive about him." Dani looked at the floor. "I think he was married or at the least had a girlfriend. I'm sure Ruth would have told me more, otherwise."

"And you don't know his name?"

Dani shook her head. "Did he do this? Did that new boyfriend kill Ruth? Did she find out he actually was married?"

I held up my hands. "It's too early to know anything. Like we said, we don't have a positive ID on the victim yet. Do you know of a woman named Deena Norman? Had Ruth ever mentioned her name?"

"Doesn't sound familiar, but if Ruth knew her well enough, the number would be on her phone."

I nodded. "Who is Ruth's next of kin, and why didn't they report her missing?"

Dani huffed. "Her mom passed away two years ago from cancer, and her dad is a loser. He never calls her."

"No siblings?"

"Yeah, a brother who she only talks to on holidays and birthdays. He lives in New Orleans."

"His name?" Renz asked.

"Kevin."

"Would you happen to have his phone number?"

"No, but that number, too, would be on Ruth's phone or somewhere in her desk." Dani teared up again. "The body is Ruth's. I just know it. She would have called me otherwise. My best friend in the entire world is dead."

I didn't have the heart to tell her there wasn't a body, but that also made me wonder who would take care of Ruth's final expenses or what the process was when Hazmat had to dispose of remains. It was something I needed to ask.

Whoever Chief Taylor assigned to go through Ruth's house would need to see if she had a will. They would also have to locate her phone to see if there was any reference to that new boyfriend. I was champing at the bit to find out who he was and have a talk with him.

I gave Dani my card, then we thanked her and left. We had to let Rita know that Deena was indeed one of the Janes being held at the medical examiner's office in Roanoke. Rita would have to arrange everything going forward as far as

Deena was concerned. We didn't have to keep Deena's body any longer, and we had plenty of photographs to consult if we needed to. Renz and I would take care of searching Deena's house since anything of importance that we found could lead us to the killer—or a connection between Deena and the other victims.

Chapter 26

Before stopping by the police station, we headed to the crime lab. Connie Jones, one of the forensic techs, went over the DNA comparison between Rita and our Jane who was found at the stream. Statistics showed that children and parents had a fifty percent DNA match, and Rita was definitely Jane's mother. From now on, Jane would be called Deena Norman, not Jane Doe number two. The DNA of Linda Thompson's uncle didn't match Jane number one, so I needed to press harder on the person who'd filed the missing persons report for Lorraine Tilley. If I had to, I would visit her in person. Later, I'd go through the most recent reports to see if any new ones had come in since we still didn't have an identity on the woman found in the Lynchburg dumpster.

We suddenly had so much to do that I knew I needed to write things down in order of urgency. First, we had to tell Rita that Deena had been identified. We also wanted to question her about Deena's friendships, or lack thereof, and find out if Deena had ever talked about anyone bothering her. Even people or incidents mentioned in innocent mother-and-daughter conversation might actually be clues that we could follow up on.

We thanked Connie and left the crime lab with copies of the reports, which I had put into my briefcase. During the drive to the police department, I dialed Rita's number.

"Do you want me to pull over during the call?" Renz asked.

I shook my head. "Nope. It doesn't matter what *we're* doing. It's the telling her that's tough."

I set the phone to Speaker and tapped the keys, and Rita picked up on the third ring.

"Hello."

"Rita, it's Agent Monroe calling. We have news from Forensics about your hair samples."

Her voice quivered as she spoke. "Okay, what were the results?"

"I'm sorry to say that they were a DNA match with our Jane Doe. The woman who was discovered at the Green Hill stream is indeed Deena. You have my deepest condolences."

Rita coughed through the phone line. "I need to process this, Agent Monroe. Right now, I can't think."

"I understand, but we need to know what Deena's occupation was, then we'll talk more tomorrow."

Rita blew her nose then responded. "She was a commercial real estate agent."

I wrote that down. "Thank you, Rita. You have my information, so please call me tomorrow, and we'll talk. I'll walk you through the process going forward, but we need to find Deena's killer, so the more we learn about Deena from you, the better. One more thing, Rita."

"Yes?"

"We need to look for evidence of anything suspicious in Deena's home. May we have your permission to do that, and did Deena keep a key outside?"

"Yes, go ahead, but please don't remove anything without discussing it with me first, and the key is under the third flowerpot on her porch."

"Okay, thank you."

The line went dead, and Rita had hung up. I glanced at Renz, and he shook his head.

"Let's give her a little breathing space. We have to question her anyway, but right now, she needs time to herself."

"I know, and it'll be just as sad if we're able to identify the other women."

We arrived at the police station and met with the chief in his office.

After being seated, Renz took the lead. "Have you spoken with the hazmat team?" he asked.

"I have," the chief said. "They've disposed of the remains but first allowed Forensics to take the samples they needed as long as they were in approved containers."

"What exactly—"

Chief Taylor looked my way. "Do they do with the remains? If they're biological, they either neutralize the material with steam or they incinerate it."

I grimaced, and I was thankful that Ruth didn't have a family who loved and cherished her. I doubted that Forensics could get viable DNA from the remains, but I had an idea to run by them.

"Have you had any luck with Lorraine Tilley or the woman found in the Lynchburg dumpster?" the chief asked.

With a nod, I responded. "We'll be working on that more this afternoon. You are aware that Deena Norman was identified, correct?"

"Yes, Forensics informed me. So, we have two more unidentified women in the morgue and one more that Hazmat had to dispose of."

"That's correct," Renz said, "but there's no evidence that the bathtub case is related to the others."

"I'll have my guys work that case, then, exclusively so you can focus on the Jane Does."

"I assume your detectives will go through Ruth's house?"

"Of course, Agent Monroe, and they'll follow up on the tip-line leads too."

"Good. Have them pass that on to us later if something looks promising."

"Will do."

I continued. "We did interview Dani Simpson, Ruth's best friend, but your team may want to conduct an interview of their own."

"And I'll make sure they do, along with talking to the neighbors once the air quality is deemed normal again."

I gave Renz a nod then stood. "So, we should continue our investigation into Janes one and three. We'll touch base with you in the morning, Chief Taylor."

As soon as Renz got behind the wheel, I told him the plan. "We aren't going back to the hotel's business center right now."

"Then where are we going?"

"To Clarksville. I want to know why that friend of Lorraine's has the wherewithal to report her missing but isn't concerned enough to return my calls."

"Do we know she'll be home?"

"No, but surprising someone is the best way to catch them at home. If I left a message that we were on our way, she'd probably make sure to be gone when we got there."

"Isn't Clarksville two and a half hours away?"

"Yeah. So? I'll camp on her doorstep if I have to."

Renz chuckled. "Okay, but you're driving."

We switched places, and I headed out after reminding Renz he had to act as copilot. "Plug her address into your GPS and take your phone off of Bluetooth so the directions go through the car's navigation."

"Yes, ma'am."

I grinned. "I want to know why the heck that woman hasn't returned my calls. It doesn't seem normal unless she has something to hide."

"Why get involved at all, then, if she had something to hide?"

"That's what I intend to find out." I glanced at the gas gauge. "We need to fill up first and then be on our way."

"And what about Deena's house?"

"We'll go through Danville when we head back to Roanoke, so we can search it then."

"Sounds like a plan to me."

I pulled into the nearest gas station and turned toward Renz. "Fill her up, partner, and I'll grab the snacks."

Chapter 27

It was late afternoon by the time we arrived at the home of Pam Hanson.

I looked across the street and up at the second-floor unit of the duplex. From what I had read, Pam lived at 202B Franklin Street. It had to be the upper apartment.

"I see a light on in the room facing us," I said.

"That's a good sign. Shall we?"

"Yep."

We left the car, stepped off the curb, and crossed the street.

"This might be tricky."

"Why?" Renz asked.

"Well, all she has to do is wait us out. She doesn't have to answer the door." I turned the knob for the upper unit—locked. Then I cupped my face with my hands and peeked through the door's window. "Shit. The stairs go immediately up to a closed door at the top. We can't go any farther than right here, the porch."

"May as well get her attention." Renz jammed his index finger into the buzzer and held it there. "We didn't drive this far just to be ignored. There was plenty of work we could have gotten accomplished if she had answered the phone."

"True, but as long as we're here, we should search Lorraine's house too."

"No can do. We don't have proof that she's dead or a verbal consent from a next of kin to enter her home."

"Yeah, yeah. Wishful thinking."

Renz pressed the buzzer again but to no avail. "Now what?"

"Damn it, I know she's home. What's the deal with that woman anyway?"

With a huff, Renz pressed the buzzer of the lower unit.

"What are you doing?"

"Getting somebody's attention. That's what."

Seconds later, a woman who looked to be in her mid-fifties opened the door. "May I help you?"

Renz pulled out his badge. "Ma'am, we're FBI agents who have been trying to get in touch with Pam Hanson. It appears that she doesn't want to talk to us. Do you have any idea why that might be?"

"No. She's my tenant, but we aren't close. Did she commit a crime? If she did, she'll have to move out. I don't want any trouble."

"Ma'am, we need to speak with Pam about a friend of hers, not about Pam herself."

"Oh… um. I guess I can unlock the lower door, then you can go upstairs and knock on the upper one." She smiled. "Maybe the buzzer isn't working."

Renz raised his brow and gave me a glance. "That would be very helpful."

We both knew the buzzer worked fine since we'd heard it clearly when Renz pressed it. I assumed a little close-up conversation through the door might help convince Pam to allow us in. We did have our means of persuasion.

With the lower door unlocked, we thanked the landlady and walked to the top of the stairs. Renz gave the door three hard raps.

"Pam Hanson, it's the FBI. We need to speak with you about Lorraine Tilley. May we come in?"

"Leave me alone. It was a mistake on my part to report her missing. I was hurt and angry."

"So, you're saying she isn't missing anymore?" I asked. "Do you have proof of that, and if you do, why didn't you cancel the missing persons report?"

We waited through a minute of silence, then Renz spoke up again. "We can talk inside your apartment privately or publicly at the Clarksville PD. Your choice."

As I heard the doorknob turn, I looked at it. She finally opened the door.

"Come in. Is it legal for the nosy bitch downstairs to let you into my apartment?"

"Actually, she didn't. She allowed us into an entryway, and she owns the property, so I guess it's legal."

Renz and I walked in, and Pam pointed at the kitchen table. "Go ahead and sit down."

We did.

"I'm Agent Monroe, and I've left you three messages. We wouldn't have had to drive two and a half hours if you had returned my calls."

"Sorry, but I've decided to back off."

I frowned. "Back off of what?"

"Lorraine. She can do her own thing if that's what she really wants. I'll quit calling and banging on her door. I don't want to look pathetic and desperate."

"Are you and Lorraine—"

"A couple? I thought so, but I guess we aren't. I saw her on several occasions with a man, and they looked very cozy. After I couldn't reach her for days, I finally reported her missing. Maybe she just wants me to leave her alone. Maybe she moved in with the guy. I don't know. The only thing I do know is that she isn't home, she doesn't answer her door, and she doesn't return my calls."

I cocked my head.

"Sorry. I guess I'm no different," Pam said.

"Doesn't Lorraine have a job?"

"Yeah, sure."

"And have you tried her there?"

"No. Like I said, I don't want to appear desperate."

"Where does she work?"

"At Lewis Dermatology here in Clarksville."

"You do realize it's been nearly two weeks since you filed that report."

Pam nodded. "I know."

I pulled out my phone, looked up the number, and called. "Hello, I'm looking for Lorraine Tilley. Can you connect me with her, please?" I listened silently as the woman on the other end of the line explained that Lorraine had quit her job via an email two weeks prior. I thanked her and hung up.

"Sounds like Lorraine quit her job several weeks ago. How would she make ends meet without working?"

"Maybe she got a new job in Danville."

Renz's frown nearly caused his eyebrows to touch. "Danville? Why there?"

"Because that's where I followed her to the first time I suspected she was seeing someone. She met a man downtown, and they drove away together."

"Have any idea what his name is?" I asked.

"No, but he drives a white Mercedes, and I can't compete with that."

I sighed. "Do you have a key to Lorraine's house?"

"I did, but she asked for it back six months ago when we got into an argument. Maybe that's when she started seeing that man. She might have decided that our kind of relationship wasn't working for her."

"What about family? Who is Lorraine's next of kin?"

Pam shrugged. "She never talked about family with me. It was just the two of us, even though that sounds cliché."

I stood and pulled two cards from my pocket. "Will you write Lorraine's address on the back of this one? You can keep the other. Call me anytime if something else comes to light."

Pam stared at the card. "Thank you, Agent Monroe, and I'm sorry you drove so far."

We left and headed to Lorraine's house. After parking, the first thing I did was check the mailbox. Letters, flyers, and junk mail filled a space the size of a bread loaf. That in itself sent a chill up my spine.

"May I help you, young lady?"

I looked left and right while trying to track the location of the voice.

"Over here on the rocking chair next door."

A woman waved her hand, then I called out to Renz. "Let's see what the neighbor knows."

We walked to the house on our left and up the steps.

The old woman wagged a bony finger at me. "It's a federal crime to snoop in somebody's mailbox, you know."

I smiled. "Then it's a good thing we're federal agents." I held out my lanyard-mounted badge.

"Open mouth, insert foot."

Renz chuckled. "Any sightings of Lorraine lately?"

"Nope, she vanished as fast as a cool summer breeze. One day she's here, and the next day she's gone. Haven't seen her in two weeks. I've taken some of her mail inside my house for when she comes home, but no luck yet."

"So, you've snooped in her mailbox?"

"Touché." She stuck out her hand and shook mine then Renz's. "I like you. The name's Edna."

"And I'm Jade, and he is Lorenzo. May we ask you some questions about Lorraine?"

"Sure. Grab a chair."

Edna seemed outgoing and welcoming. I imagined she didn't have regular visitors. I also imagined she enjoyed talking, and that was good for us. When Renz began, her eyes lit up.

"So, Edna, were you and Lorraine close?"

"Yeah, she was a nice girl. I miss having peach iced tea with her here on the porch. I just don't understand why she would pick up and leave without so much as a goodbye. I thought we were friends."

"That does sound odd," I said. "Do you know Pam?"

"Her lady friend?"

"Yes, that Pam. She said she came by several times looking for Lorraine, but she never found her."

Edna shook her head. "I don't agree with that lifestyle, but it's none of my business. There were times, though, that I could hear them arguing through Lorraine's open window." Edna looked both ways then whispered. "I did see a man here a few times. His car sat right down there." She pointed a thin shaky finger at a spot down the street.

"He didn't park in front of the house?"

"No, ma'am. I think they had a secret thing going on, if you know what I mean."

I nodded. "Do you remember anything about that man's car, Edna?"

"Yes, it was fancy and white."

"Did Lorraine ever talk about the man?" Renz asked.

"Not a word. She knew I wouldn't approve while she was in a relationship—even if it was with another woman. In my time, that was called stepping out."

"Or cheating, right?"

"Yes, Miss Jade, or cheating."

"Other than the occasional argument between Lorraine and Pam, have you ever heard screaming and cries for help or seen unusual commotion going on next door?"

When Renz addressed her, Edna's eyes danced. "No, sir, Lorenzo. Not a peep. I will say your name reminds me of a

Casanova—a Spanish lover, a dancer. One who charms the ladies." She sighed. "If only I was thirty again."

I grinned as Renz's face went red. Edna was easily distracted by him and his handsome Spanish features. She was clearly smitten.

We stood, and I gave Renz a raised brow. "Go ahead and give Edna your card, just in case Lorraine comes home." I took Edna by her frail hand. Her skin was thin but soft. "We sure appreciate your help, Edna. By the way, Pam said it was okay if we just looked around outside a little."

"Okay, dear, and it was nice speaking with you." She smiled at Renz. "And you, too, Lorenzo."

As we crossed the yard to Lorraine's house, I elbowed Renz in the ribs. "Since when would an old lady have the hots for you?"

"Charm has no boundaries, and lust has no age limits."

I laughed as we tried to peer into Lorraine's blind-covered windows. We did the same at each window around the house but couldn't see inside. "Do we know what kind of car Lorraine drove?"

"I don't think it was in the police report, and I haven't checked the DMV records yet," Renz said.

"Well, either you can give me a boost so I can look through those windows at the top of the garage door, or you can go back and ask Edna."

Renz looked me up and down. "What do you weigh?"

My mouth curled up in a smile. "A buck twenty-five. Now make up your mind."

He entwined his fingers and stood against the garage

door. "Step into my hand, and you better get a good look. I don't want to do this a dozen times."

"Yes, Casanova." I wedged my fingers between the spaces in the door and stepped up. It was dark in the single-car garage, but I could definitely see the shape of a vehicle. I jumped down. "Renz, there's a car inside."

"You sure? It isn't a golf cart or something like that?"

I contorted my face. "No, and why the hell would she have a golf cart? There isn't a golf course nearby, and this doesn't look like one of those golf cart communities. I'm telling you it's a car."

"Okay, okay. I've got to call Taft. She might want us to go inside. I think that would fit into the 'probable cause to search' rationale more than the 'running away with a boyfriend' scenario."

We returned to the car, where Renz made the call and set the phone to Speaker.

"Hey, Boss, it's Lorenzo."

"What's the latest?" Maureen asked.

"Well, we're in a predicament that you'll have to make the decision on."

"Okay, shoot."

Renz told Taft that we were sitting outside Lorraine Tilley's house and that there was a car in the garage yet nobody had seen her in weeks. Renz shared what the woman who reported Lorraine missing had recounted, noting that after some thought, she believed Lorraine was seeing a man in Danville and hadn't actually disappeared.

"How far is Danville from Clarksville?"

"An hour," I said.

"That isn't far enough away to abandon your home or vehicle. Something happened to her."

"And her workplace said she quit two weeks ago via an email," I said.

"Yep, smells fishy to me. Who's the Danville man?"

"We didn't get a name, only that he has a white Mercedes."

"Okay, get with the Clarksville PD and tell them you need them to meet you at the home for a wellness check. That could bypass the warrant to get inside the house. Try to get in without breaking down the door and call me back if you find anything. Remember, we don't have a warrant, so no digging through everything. Have a look and leave."

"Yes, ma'am," Renz said before hanging up. He turned to me. "Go ask Edna if she knows where Lorraine kept a key."

"Why don't you? She's putty in your hands."

"Because I don't want to linger there, now go."

I huffed at his lack of humor. "Fine, then you call the PD."

I returned to Edna's porch. She glanced past me, and I saw her look of hope fading quickly.

"No Lorenzo?"

"Sorry, but he had to make a call to the police department. Edna, do you know if Lorraine kept a house key hidden outside?"

"Well, I believe she did, but *where* is another question. My mind isn't as good as it used to be."

"Maybe under something or somewhere on the porch?"

"Yes, that's it. She hid it under the leg of the porch bench."

"Great! Thank you, Edna. Don't be alarmed, but the police are going to walk us through Lorraine's house just to make sure everything is okay."

"Then take her mail inside while you're at it. Hold on while I get the rest."

I wasn't there to be the mail person, but if it made Edna feel better, I would do it. She returned to the porch seconds later with a plastic grocery bag full of mail. I thanked her and left. I knew she was watching, so I made a quick stop at the mailbox, filled the bag with everything that was jammed inside the box, then headed for Lorraine's house. I glanced to my left, saw Edna nod her approval, and nodded back.

"What the hell are you doing?" Renz asked when I reached the porch.

I swatted the air. "Edna insisted that I take Lorraine's mail inside. When will the police be here?"

"Any minute. Do we know of a key?"

"Oh yeah, it's under one of the bench legs."

Renz lifted the bench and found a key beneath the back right leg. "Humph. Edna has a good memory for an old gal." He slid the key into the doorknob slot, and it fit perfectly. "The right key for the right door. That's a plus."

Chapter 28

Seconds later, a squad car pulled to the curb. The officer inside killed the engine and stepped out. From the passenger side, another officer exited the vehicle, then they both walked toward us.

"We need a wellness check here?"

"That's correct," Renz said as he showed the officers his badge. "We have a key, but the entry needs to be done officially and on the books. There's also a vehicle in the garage even though the resident was reported missing weeks ago."

"Sure thing, Agent DeLeon. Whenever you're ready."

Renz noted the time then turned the key in the knob. The door squeaked open. I realized I was instinctively holding my breath. Cautiously, I let it out then inhaled. No odor of death—a plus anytime we entered a home.

I hung the bag of mail over the coat closet's doorknob. At first glance, the home appeared absolutely normal. We didn't see signs of a struggle, nothing looked out of place, and no chairs were tipped or drawers pulled out.

Maybe Lorraine did leave everything behind and disappear,

but why didn't she take her car? Why not move out? Why not sell the home? It made no sense, and like Taft said, it smelled fishy.

We gloved up in case the home actually was a crime scene that had been cleaned, then we walked the house. Renz asked the officers to check the garage and call in the car's plates to make sure it belonged to Lorraine Tilley.

They went to the garage, and Renz and I headed down the hallway. We were in a typical two-bedroom, one-bath home, the perfect size for a single person. The house appeared neat and clean. Only a slight musty smell lingered, likely from being closed up and having days of torrential rain during the week of the hurricane.

I snapped pictures as we looked at items in each room, but I kept Taft's reminder in mind—no digging through things.

"See anything suspicious?" I asked as Renz opened the master closet.

"Yeah, three suitcases. If she went somewhere for an extended period of time, wouldn't she have packed a suitcase or two?"

I peered around his shoulder and took a look. "One would think." I snapped a picture with my phone, and we continued on.

"See a phone charger anywhere?" Renz asked.

I looked in the typical places—the nightstand, on the desk, on the end table next to the couch, then finally, on the kitchen counter.

"Bingo. An empty charger. Either the phone is wherever

she is, or it got tossed. Come to think of it, I haven't seen a purse either."

The officers came back into the house through the laundry room that connected to the garage.

"We have the details on the car. It's a 2019 Honda Accord, and it's registered to Lorraine Tilley."

"Does it have Navigation?" I asked.

"It looks that way according to the characters on the steering wheel, but of course we'd need the key to light up the infotainment center to be sure."

Renz frowned. "Why does that matter?"

"Maybe she programmed destinations into it. When she met up with that Danville man for the first time, she might have used it."

Renz nodded. "Not a bad idea, but we'd have to find the car key."

"Right, and it's probably on her key ring in her invisible purse." I raised my index finger. "Although, everyone gets two sets of keys when they buy a car. The second set, at least from my personal experience, gets thrown in the junk drawer." My eyes darted around the kitchen.

Renz wagged his index finger at me. "Taft said no digging."

"I won't be digging, just browsing and for a good cause."

Renz rolled his eyes but pitched in anyway by opening and closing kitchen drawers. All we needed were the car keys, and with them, we might find out everything we needed to know.

It took only a minute to locate the junk drawer, and with a pencil, I moved items around until I found the second set of keys. "I've got them, Renz."

"Okay, let's get that car started and see if it holds any information."

The four of us walked to the garage. Renz suggested lifting the overhead so the exhaust wouldn't fill the small area with fumes.

We didn't know whether a crime had been committed there, but we currently had nothing to warrant a forensic team coming to the house. We would see if the navigation system could give us clues to work with. If not, we'd lock up the house again and leave. Unless we found proof that Lorraine was dead, our hands were tied, but if a thorough search was warranted later, Forensics could dust the house for prints, and the Clarksville PD could search it.

I smiled nervously at Renz. "The moment of truth."

He turned the key, and the infotainment center came to life. Renz pressed the locations button on the navigation screen and gave me a look of disappointment.

I punched the dash. "You've got to be kidding! There's absolutely nothing on there."

Renz shrugged. "A lot of people use their phone for navigating, Jade. It's not unusual to bypass a car's system and use your phone instead. We do it all the time."

I couldn't argue with that. We did do it all the time because we were familiar with our phones. Every car we had rented was different, and programming an address into an unfamiliar car's navigation system meant time wasted. Phones were fast and easy.

"Well, shit."

Renz shut down the car, we gave it a quick look through

and found nothing, then he handed me the spare key. "Put it back where you found it." He looked at the officers. "I guess we're done here. No crime that I can see, and no dead body in the house. You can just write down that the welfare check went without incident and the resident wasn't home."

The officers left, and we promised to follow up with the Clarksville PD and tell the captain there why we'd needed to enter the home and what we had found—nothing suspicious.

Renz lowered the overhead, and we returned to the kitchen. A wall calendar hung from a short nail on the side of the cabinet. I hadn't noticed it before, but when I moved in closer, I saw daily events written on it.

"Renz, take a look at this. This is damn near a diary of Lorraine's comings and goings over the year so far."

"Holy shit. That could prove significant."

Still gloved, I took down the calendar, placed it on the counter, and looked through the previous month's entries. I jabbed the ones that could be important.

"Look. There are times and locations noted on dates going back months. Maybe they're secret rendezvous with that mystery man. No names are shown, but if Lorraine was still with Pam at the time, that's probably why. Should we take it?"

"You know we can't."

"Well, I'll take pictures, then, since I can do whatever I want with my phone. These dates could be crucial in finding out what happened to Lorraine." I thought about her brother. "What we really need is a DNA match, and Kevin doesn't sound like a reliable source." I rubbed my chin as I thought. "Wait! If Lorraine didn't leave voluntarily, then that means her hairbrush and toothbrush should still be here." I ran to the bathroom and saw a clean countertop. There wasn't even a toothbrush holder sitting there. "It's got to be in the drawer."

"What does?" Renz asked when he crowded into the bathroom alongside me.

"Her toothbrush or hairbrush." I pulled open the top drawer and found a bonanza of items we could get DNA from. "Shit. The officers left, and we need to bag this stuff to be tested."

"I'll find something in the kitchen." Renz pointed. "There's a toothbrush. Looks like an electric one, but why isn't the base on the counter?"

"Who knows? Maybe she didn't like clutter, but I'll grab that and her hairbrush."

Seconds later, Renz was back with two quart-sized zipper bags. "These will work." He looked in the drawer. "Anything else?"

"Nah, these should be enough to test against Jane number one. With proof that Jane is Lorraine and by using those locations, dates, and times on the calendar pictures I took, we should be able to find out what she did and what her plans were before she disappeared."

Renz nodded. "And with whom."

With each month of the calendar photographed and the plastic bag in hand, I shut off the lights and stepped outside. Renz locked up and placed the key back under the bench leg, then we returned to the car.

It was already getting late, and we had a long way to go.

"Maybe we should check out Deena's house tomorrow in the daylight. I wouldn't want someone calling the police, thinking we were prowlers. Plus, I'd like to drop off these samples at the crime lab, and hopefully, the night crew can get a head start on them."

"Sounds like a smart plan. We'll grab something from a drive-through at the halfway point."

It was after nine o'clock by the time we got back to Roanoke. We made a stop at the forensic lab before heading to the hotel and calling it a night. They promised to get started on the DNA matches immediately. If luck was on our side, we would have Deena and Lorraine positively identified. Hopefully, Ruth would be identified as well if they could get DNA from that piece of peach-colored clothing or a remaining hair strand and match it to something in her house.

That left the Lynchburg dumpster woman for us to identify, along with the person who we assumed was the killer and had the initials DM. We'd already eliminated the doctor from Danville since he'd been out of town for the entire two weeks the murders were taking place.

We still had to figure out why the word "slut" was carved into the women's faces. That signaled that the killer was somebody who was either obsessed with something those women possessed or did, or jealous of their physical appearance. The latter made me think of something I needed to discuss with Renz.

Chapter 29

It was Chris's only weekend to complete the mission and cross every name off the list. After that, and with the car packed and a new destination in rural Vermont already secured, Chris would disappear for good.

There was no monetary gain from killing five people, but the emotional satisfaction was worth a lot. In time, after the will was read, Chris was sure that money would be coming in. Even though the business had been bought years before Chris was in the picture, there were always exceptions to the rule. Successful businesses took time and expensive attorneys to dissolve, so committing the murders quickly, before things could change, was the only way to insure financial gain down the road.

Months had gone by, and Chris wasn't accustomed to pinching pennies and living in a two-bit apartment in a two-bit town, but playing the game and being patient would be rewarding in the long run. The last murder would guarantee that.

So far, the police had nothing. The news broadcasts about the unidentified women had all but fizzled out, and nothing came up online. If any tip-line leads had been worthwhile, the cops would have been knocking on Chris's door.

Scot-free and without suspicion, just the way I like it. Nobody has a clue who those women are, and calling in multiple false reports of women who have gone missing just adds to the mess the police have to follow up on.

Chris had the code to the guard gate and a key to the house. Those were the only items necessary—except for a weapon to commit the last murder with.

No guns. Too easy to trace, yet I have to take into consideration who I'm dealing with. I could hire someone to do the dirty work, but then I'd have to pay him, and I can't pay in advance. Plus, there would be a paper trail and another person involved who might blackmail me. Anything that needs to stay quiet needs to be done alone. Loose lips sink ships or, in other words, me.

Chris knew what time the next victim would get home, and lying in wait was the only way to take him down successfully. Blindsides worked—period.

Chapter 30

"Want to call it a night or wrap up today's events over a drink or two? The restaurant is open until eleven," Renz said as we neared the hotel.

I chuckled. "Yeah, I could use a glass of wine or three."

Renz pulled up to the restaurant and cut the engine. I was ready to relax after a long day, plus discussing the cuts on the women's cheeks over a glass of wine sounded good. Maybe the marks held more clues that we hadn't thought of yet.

After we were seated, I looked around. A handful of people were scattered throughout the space, giving me the freedom to say what I needed as long as I kept my voice down. We made small talk until the waitress arrived with our bottle of Chianti, crusty bread, and dipping oil to share over our nightly conversation.

"Renz, we need to dig deeper into the cheek carvings."

He wrinkled his brow. "Okay, I'll bite. What's on your mind?"

"Well, we already know the first initials stand for the women's names. That's been proven with Deena and most likely Lorraine too."

Renz nodded then leaned in closer.

I took a sip of wine then continued. "But we've never delved into the reason the word 'slut' is carved into their cheek."

"Sounds like something a pissed-off person writes."

"Yes, of course, but he completely destroyed their faces."

"Hmm…"

My brows shot up. "Hmm, what?"

"I think we're looking at this all wrong. Why would a man carve 'slut' into random women's faces? I mean, we still have to question Rita to find out if Deena knew Lorraine, but because they didn't share the same occupation or live in the same town, there's no reason to assume they did."

"Yeah, go on," I said.

"In my mind, that's something a woman would call another woman."

My head nearly blew off my shoulders.

Renz continued. "To me, it sounds like jealousy, sour grapes, an envious person, hatred, etcetera. And—"

I jumped in. "And that's why the women's faces are cut beyond recognition. It has to be something about their faces. Too beautiful, maybe?"

"Maybe the killer is disfigured or just ugly and is taking out their rage on random women."

I shook my head. "I doubt that they're random women. The killer chose them for a reason only they can justify. Otherwise, she could have found a homeless woman to kill. They were middle-class hardworking ladies. Deena was a real estate agent, Lorraine worked at a dermatology clinic, and Ruth was a paralegal."

Renz raised his hands. "I doubt that Ruth is part of this killing spree. The MO is all wrong."

I shrugged. "Just saying. We still need to find out who the dumpster woman in Lynchburg is too. I'll contact Captain Reynolds in the morning to see if he has any updates. After that, I'll go through the most recent missing persons reports again." I let out a groan then took a full gulp of wine and refilled my glass. "So, if a woman is actually the killer, then that changes everything. I have to admit, you're correct about the word 'slut,' Renz. That would be something a woman would say more than a man. A man wouldn't have a reason to carve 'slut' on a woman's face unless she was his wife or girlfriend and he found out she was cheating."

Renz shook his head. "Yet that word was on the faces of three women, not just one. So…"

"So what?"

"So, I'm thinking out loud, and I'll admit I'm kind of stumped."

I pulled in a long breath to clear my head. "Okay, three women for sure with initials and the word 'slut' carved into their faces. DMMD on all of their right cheeks. Three women, one man? That's it, Renz! It has to be. The person who killed Deena, Lorraine, and the woman in Lynchburg is either the wife or the girlfriend of a man who was cheating on her with all of them. She's pointing the finger at him as if saying he's the reason she killed them. It's his fault she went that far."

"I think you're onto something, Jade. We finally could be barking up the right tree."

We polished off the wine and called it a night. My mind was in full gear, so I knew I would have a hard time sleeping.

Back in my room, I downed a melatonin tablet, took a hot shower, and made my nightly call to Amber. I ran the scenario past her, and she wholeheartedly agreed that the killer was likely a scorned woman.

With that affirmation, I had a sense of hope. Tomorrow, we could run our idea by Taft, get her take on it, and go from there. A thought was percolating, and I planned to share it with Renz over breakfast, but for now, I had to do my best to fall asleep.

Chapter 31

I woke that Saturday morning with renewed enthusiasm even though at five days in, we still didn't have a name to attach to the killer.

That's going to change and damn soon.

I rose, started the coffee, and turned on the TV. As I picked out my clothes for the day, the morning news had an update coming from Lynchburg. I stopped what I was doing, paused the TV, and poured a cup of coffee. After resuming the news, I gave the segment my full attention.

A witness had finally come forward after nearly a week and given the police a statement.

"Holy shit. This can break open the case."

I paused the TV again and called Renz's phone.

"Are you awake?" I asked the second the ringing stopped. Renz hadn't even said hello yet.

"I am now. What has you all jacked up?"

"Hurry and turn on your TV to channel seven." I heard Renz fumbling with the remote.

"Yeah, okay. It's on. What am I looking at?"

"You probably can't back it up because you just turned it

on. My TV is paused, so I can start the segment over if you want to come over here to see all of it."

"Give me two minutes and have a cup of coffee waiting. What the hell is the segment about?"

"The Lynchburg Jane Doe."

"Shit. I'll be there in one minute."

My clothes from yesterday were good enough for the time being. I would dress for the day after Renz watched the segment with me. After I slipped on my pants and zipped them, he banged on my door. I pulled it open, invited him in, then handed him a cup of coffee.

"Sit and watch." I poured myself another coffee then took a seat next to Renz at the table. "Ready?"

"Hell yeah. Let's see what they found."

I pressed the forward arrow, and the segment began with an image of the Day N' Night Drive-In. Seconds into it, a shot of the dumpsters and the EMTs came into view. I was sure those images had been captured by reporters who were ordered to stay behind the yellow crime scene tape that fateful night.

Renz blew over his coffee then took a sip. "Okay, okay, get to the part we don't know."

The anchor continued by saying that after nearly a week of silence, a witness had come forward and given police a statement. That witness, who wanted to stay anonymous, was interviewed off-camera, and their voice was altered.

The newsperson was told the witness had spoken to the police and wouldn't go to the media. He wanted to remain unnamed and unseen. The anchorman said the witness wasn't even certain that he saw a crime being committed until the news had spread throughout Lynchburg and he connected the dots.

I took that to mean that either the witness was young and afraid, or the killer actually knew they had been seen committing the crime.

I was sure the news didn't have the entire story and could only report what the police allowed them to know. According to what they were told, the anchor said, the witness was cutting through the alley on his way to work early that morning and heard the loud bang of the dumpster lid being flung open. He then saw a dark figure open the back of a vehicle, heave a large bag over their shoulder, and toss it into the can. The figure spun around when they heard a noise, locked eyes with the witness for a second, then climbed back into their vehicle and sped away.

The witness said he thought the person was dumping a bunch of trash and didn't want anyone to know since the dumpster wasn't a public-use container. It wasn't until days later that he realized what he'd witnessed.

A commercial break came on, then the local Roanoke news followed.

"I'm going to call Reynolds and find out what the hell really happened."

Renz frowned. "It's a quarter after seven. You want to let the guy get out of bed before you start interrogating him? I'm sure he intended to get ahold of us. What I figure is that the cops know what kind of vehicle the killer climbed into and, with any luck, somewhat of a description of them too."

"Let's hope so, and let's hope that witness got a license plate number as well."

Renz chuckled. "If you saw someone toss what you thought was trash into a dumpster, would you think to snap off a picture of their license plate?"

"Of course I would." I frowned. "Okay, I wouldn't, but no matter what, it's imperative that we talk to that witness today."

Renz finished his coffee and headed for the door. "Breakfast in a half hour?"

"Yep, sounds good. Renz, you know what this means?"

He turned around. "That there's a chance we learn the identity of each victim?"

"Yes, and also the identity of the killer."

"That would make for a good Saturday."

After Renz walked out, I locked the door then took a three-minute shower. The news continued to play in the background as I dried off and dressed for the day. There wasn't any more mention of the Lynchburg Jane Doe, but that would change as soon as I talked to Reynolds. If that witness had more information, the police already knew and were working on it.

Renz and I headed out the door at seven forty-five. At eight thirty, I planned to call Captain Reynolds. I had no idea if he worked the weekend shift, but one way or another, I would get through to him.

"So," Renz said after we placed our breakfast orders. "Do you have a game plan in mind?"

"Yep. Eat, call the captain and learn the details, then head to Lynchburg and talk to that witness." I shook my head. "I've got to add to my notes, or I'll forget everything we need to do today. We have to follow up with Rita, search the missing persons database again, talk to Forensics about Lorraine being Jane number one, and—"

Renz chuckled. "And pull out your hair."

I gave him my best scowl. "It isn't funny. We're still planning to go to Deena's house, and Danville is a good distance away too."

"Sorry. I'm not making fun, but that's a lot to accomplish in one day."

"And it's par for the course. Hurry up and wait and then all the shit hits at once." I tipped my wrist and checked the time.

"We're doing fine. You're going to eat your breakfast, and then while I drive, you can make most of your calls."

The waitress headed our way carrying two cast-iron frying pans. "Here you go, two loaded omelets. I'll be right back with the toast and hash browns."

I smiled, thanked her, and poured two more coffees.

Chapter 32

After breakfast, we took ten minutes, went back to our rooms, and gathered what we needed for the day. I brushed my teeth, checked the frizz status on my hard-to-control-in-humidity hair, and with a groan, headed out the door.

In the car and on the passenger side, I snapped my seat belt, pulled out the papers I needed along with my pen, and put those items in the door pocket. Then I placed my briefcase on my lap to use as a tabletop for making calls and taking notes.

Renz pulled out of the parking lot as I organized what I needed for the calls I was about to make. The first would be to Captain Reynolds. His card, a blank sheet of paper, and my pen sat on the make-do table. Before dialing, I asked Renz if he wanted to join in on the conversation.

"Yeah, go ahead and put it on Speaker."

I did then made the call. Nobody picked up on the captain's direct line, so I called the main number.

"Lynchburg Police Department, how may I direct your call?"

"Hello, this is FBI Agent Jade Monroe calling for Captain Reynolds. Is he in this morning?"

"I'm sorry, but he isn't. Sergeant Kline has the weekend shift."

"And has Sergeant Kline been briefed about the witness coming forward in the Jane Doe dumpster murder?"

"I have no idea, ma'am. Shall I connect you to his office?"

"Yes, please." I whispered to Renz as I waited. "I hope Reynolds filled him in on our involvement."

"Sergeant Kline here."

"Hello, Sergeant Kline. This is Agent Monroe with the FBI. My partner and I just learned of a witness coming forward in the Jane Doe dumpster case."

"Yes, the captain told me to contact you this morning. Actually, I just got in."

I gave Renz a thumbs-up. "Sir, we're on our way to Lynchburg right now. We need to know everything the witness passed on, then we intend to speak with him ourselves."

"Sure on our part, but that young man is an unreliable witness. It was hard enough getting him to talk after he came in."

"We'll handle that end of things after we're briefed by you or Captain Reynolds as to where everything stands right now."

"Sorry? Nothing has changed, Agent Monroe, other than the kid saying he saw something odd that morning."

"So, he didn't give you a description of the person or the car?"

"Somewhat of one but it was too vague to get us anywhere. Nothing was handed to us on a silver platter if that's what you're asking."

"Okay, we'll discuss everything when we get there. Expect to see us in thirty minutes."

I hung up and shook my head. I wasn't sure if the Lynchburg PD realized how important the eyewitness information could be. Every clue, no matter how small, could help tie the pieces together. I couldn't wait to interview that young man.

With a half hour to go before we reached Lynchburg, I made the call to Rita. Yesterday, I had told her to call me, but from experience, I knew that grieving people rarely took that initiative. We needed to know more about Deena.

It took three rings before she answered, but when she did, she seemed ready to talk about whatever I had to ask.

"Thank you so much for picking up, Rita," I said. "There are a few things I need to ask in order to help track down Deena's killer. If you don't know the answers, that's okay, but if you do, every little bit helps."

"Yes. Go ahead, then."

"Great. First, did Deena mention anything about a man in her life?"

"She did say she recently began seeing someone, but she didn't tell me his name."

"Did she say where he was from? Danville, maybe, because she lived there too?"

"I guess I assumed that, but she didn't say so specifically."

"Okay, anything about a person who was bothering her? Threatening calls, texts, emails?"

"No, nothing like that."

"Do you know if Deena knew a Lorraine Tilley or a man named Drew Mills?"

"I've never heard either name mentioned. Keep in mind, Agent Monroe, I didn't live near Deena, so I'd have to believe whatever she wanted to share with me, and if she didn't want to share, there'd be no way I'd know."

Rita was absolutely right. Information shared in long-distance relationships—whether that was between friends, parents and children, siblings, or lovers—had to be taken at face value. There was no other way. Rita gave me names of several friends Deena had had over the years. Unless we were lucky enough to find a phone in her house later, I would have to track them down since Deena's phone had never been retrieved. I thanked Rita, promised to be in touch, and ended the call. We were closing in on Lynchburg, and Renz and I needed to discuss our upcoming meeting with Sergeant Kline.

When we arrived in Lynchburg, Renz drove straight to the police station. We would review the witness statement, discuss it with the sergeant or call Captain Reynolds, then interview the witness—skittish or not. We needed to know every detail he remembered about that morning, no matter how insignificant he might think it was.

At the front counter just beyond the entrance, Renz showed his credentials and asked for Sergeant Kline. A quick call was all it took, then the sergeant appeared in under a minute. Introductions were exchanged, then we walked with him to his office, where I noticed a folder lying on his desk.

"Please, have a seat, Agents. I took the liberty of printing out the witness statement so you'll have a copy of your own."

Surprised, I thanked him, then Renz and I silently read

the interview together. The witness, a Tyler Spencer, nineteen, had been on his way to work at a different fast-food restaurant across the street and a block away from the one where the victim was found. He and two other employees were opening that morning, and he had cut through the alley to shorten the walk. He'd told police his story days later but only after people at his own workplace were talking about it. My eyes darted across the words as I looked for something that could be a clue—color of car, make and model, what the person was wearing, height and weight, and so on. Like Kline said, the information was vague, and the only way to learn more was by pressing the witness.

Renz finished reading before I did and began questioning Kline. "So, who took the kid's statement? An officer, you, the captain, who?"

Kline tipped his head toward the paper. "I believe it says on the report."

"So, the kid was interviewed by an officer J. Goldstein? A witness who saw a possible murder suspect likely dumping a body wasn't interviewed by detectives or someone higher up the chain of command?"

"The body was discovered Monday night. According to the coroner in Roanoke, Dr. Morgan, his belief was that the body had been placed there in the early hours of Monday morning."

Renz cocked his head. "That's already been established." Renz poked the report with his finger. "And the witness was walking to work early Monday morning when he saw the incident take place. So?"

"So, the weekday crew was in charge then and also when the young man came in to give his statement. I'm not certain how interviews are handled during the week and under the command of someone else."

"But Captain Reynolds ought to know, correct?"

"I would assume so."

I frowned as I listened to their back-and-forth exchange.

Renz continued. "So, because he was young, works for a ten-dollar-an-hour wage, and since days had passed, nobody took him seriously? Is that what you think?"

"My opinion of who interviewed him doesn't matter. The interview was recorded, written down, and the proper procedures were followed, Agent DeLeon."

Renz took the sheet in hand again. "The interview took place yesterday at six p.m., yet nobody informed us. You do know this murder is part of an ongoing investigation we're working on, don't you?"

"I do, but I don't know why you weren't immediately contacted. Maybe you should speak directly with the captain since everything you're hearing from me is secondhand information."

I spoke up. "Can you get him on the line? We'll discuss this via a phone conversation, or he can come in and explain. To me, it seems like the one and only witness isn't being taken seriously."

The sergeant sighed. "The witness, Tyler Spencer, is autistic. He has the mental capacity of a twelve-year-old."

It was my turn to cock my head. "Yet he has a job and also the wherewithal to report to the police what he saw the other morning. I think he'll be just fine."

"Does Tyler live with his parents?" Renz asked.

"He does, and they're skeptical of what he saw as well."

Renz pointed his chin at the phone. "Go ahead and call the captain. Last I heard, witness statements should be taken seriously unless there's a legitimate reason to discredit them."

A half hour later, Reynolds walked into the precinct. If I read his expression correctly, he was either irritated that we wanted answers, or he was embarrassed that we had called out him and the department. We needed to know what actions were taken after Tyler reported what he had seen.

We moved into an office that had a large table at one end. We gathered around it and waited for Reynolds to speak up.

"I hear you're disgruntled that you weren't contacted immediately after our witness filled out his report."

Renz shook his head. "Being disgruntled FBI agents has nothing to do with this. We were pretty busy late yesterday and likely wouldn't have made it to Lynchburg until today anyway. Our concern is what happened after the interview took place."

"I'm not following."

"Were you here when Tyler came in?"

"Yeah, somewhere in the building."

"Were detectives here as well?"

"Of course."

"Yet a rookie cop took Tyler's statement. So, between then and now, what has the PD done to further the investigation?"

Reynolds glanced at Kline. "Well, Mike, what follow-up has the department done?"

Kline looked at the wall clock. "I've only been on duty for an hour."

"So that's a nothing?" I asked. "Did anyone press Tyler for details or just let him fill out the paperwork and go about his afternoon?"

"Um," Reynolds said. "The kid makes shit up, okay? This isn't the first time we've heard wild stories come out of his mouth."

"Did the other stories involve an ongoing murder case?" Renz asked.

The room went silent.

"I didn't think so. We need the kid's phone number, his address, and the names of his parents."

"It's in the report," Kline said.

I gave it another look. "His parents' names aren't shown."

Reynolds sighed. "Tom and Beth."

Renz and I stood. "We'll be back later," Renz said. "Meanwhile, we sure as heck hope that killer hasn't checked another innocent victim off their list."

Chapter 33

"Program the home address into your phone and let's get going. You may have enough time to check in with Forensics while I'm driving."

I tapped in the address and waited. Seconds later, the results showed a six-minute drive.

"That's doable," I said as I handed my phone to Renz. "Listen as the automated voice calls out the directions. Now, give me your phone so I can call Forensics."

He did then took a seat behind the wheel and fired up the ignition. We were off. Meanwhile, I tapped the number Renz had programmed into his phone for Roanoke's crime lab. With the phone pinned between my shoulder and ear, I pulled my notepad out of the door pocket, along with a pen, and was ready to write.

If Lorraine's DNA matched the DNA of our Jane number one, then I would tell Pam, Lorraine's estranged girlfriend. While we had tried to find a relative of Lorraine's, the search had proved unsuccessful, so Pam was her next of kin as far as I was concerned.

"Crime lab, Gavin speaking."

"Gavin, it's Agent Monroe. How are we looking for the DNA comparison between Lorraine Tilley and Jane Doe number one?"

"You didn't get Connie's message?"

"My phone could have lost cell service during our drive to Lynchburg. That's where we are now. So anyway, I didn't hear a message."

"Yeah, the samples matched, meaning Jane number one is Lorraine Tilley."

"That's great news, I guess. Sad but great only because it gets us one step closer to the killer."

"Understood."

"Okay, we'll pick up the paperwork either later tonight or tomorrow morning. Thank you, Gavin."

"You bet."

I hung up, placed Renz's phone in the cup holder, then gave him a glance. "You got the drift of that conversation, right?"

"Yep. You want to call Pam now or later?"

I shook my head. "Not now. I'll do it later when there's more time to talk."

Renz slowed to a crawl on the street Tyler lived on. My phone called out that the address was the next house on the right.

I pointed at a yellow home with green-and-white-and-black-striped awnings shading the front windows. "I guess that's the place."

Renz killed the engine. "Let's see who's home."

After parking at the curb, we walked to the front door.

Renz gave it two raps, and we waited. Seconds later, a man answered and gave us a questioning look.

"Yes?"

The man's graying hair told us he wasn't Tyler but likely his dad. Renz began by asking if he was Tom Spencer, and after getting yes as a response, he introduced us.

"I imagine this is about Tyler and his eyewitness account?"

"It is, Mr. Spencer. We've read the interview the police conducted with Tyler, but we have questions of our own."

"Since when does the FBI involve themselves with a local murder case?"

I fielded that question. "Sir, we can't go into details, but we believe this case may be related to others we're investigating. Is Tyler home?"

"He is, but his weekend shift starts in an hour."

"We won't be long." I smiled, held my ground, and mentioned that it was imperative that we speak directly with Tyler.

With what sounded like an apprehensive groan, Mr. Spencer invited us inside and into the living room. "Have a seat. I'll get him."

Voices came from the end of the hall, probably the father informing the son that he had visitors. Seconds later, Tyler walked out and took a seat across from us on the couch.

Renz thanked him for reporting what he had witnessed to the police and said we needed to question him as well.

"Tyler, can you go over the incident you saw that morning when you were walking to work? It's extremely important that we know every detail you saw and remember in case the police didn't document all of it."

"I told them everything."

"So, you described the vehicle and the person to them?" I asked. "There wasn't much about it on the report."

He frowned. "It was still dark outside. Everything was the same color."

I smiled. "And that's okay. Did you happen to see a model name on the vehicle, or even a flash of color?"

Tyler closed his eyes and scrunched his face. "Um. I saw the color when the person sped by under the alley light. I was walking the same way they were going."

"And what was that color?"

"Red."

"Red? That's great. Do you know a lot about cars, Tyler?" Renz asked.

He shrugged. "No."

"Would you be able to tell the difference between a car, a truck, a van, or an SUV?"

"Yeah, I know that."

I was hopeful. "Okay, and when that red vehicle passed under the light, could you tell what kind of vehicle it was?"

"It was a Jeep."

Renz nodded. "So, an SUV or a truck?"

"No, a Jeep."

Mr. Spencer spoke up. "Tyler has always liked Jeeps, so he's kind of stuck on them. He thinks everything is a Jeep."

I temporarily ignored the father. "You saw a red Jeep, Tyler?"

"Yeah. Don't I need to go to work, Dad?"

"Yes, soon."

I continued. "Did you see the person very well, Tyler? The police said you told them that they had a large garbage bag over their shoulder that they tossed into the dumpster."

"They did."

"But if that bag contained a body, don't you think it would have been heavy?"

"I suppose so, but that's what I saw."

"Okay, and then that person noticed you, right?"

He nodded. "That's when they got back in the Jeep and drove off."

"Was that person tall, husky, skinny, or muscular?"

"Tall and husky, with a ponytail."

Renz wrinkled his face. "The man had a ponytail?"

"No. It was a woman. She did."

Chapter 34

After parking a block away, Chris entered the all-too-familiar house on Sunrise Street and locked the door behind her. Ten months had passed since she had been there, inside what used to be her home, her sanctuary, her happy place. The house held hundreds of memories, some good but more that were bad.

She took the stairs to the second floor and entered the master bedroom. It had changed. More women than Chris cared to count had slept in that bed since she'd left. Since she'd been thrown out. Since she wasn't desirable anymore.

Chris opened the drapes, unlocked the glass door, and stepped out. The balcony faced east, and viewing the morning sunrise over coffee was something that always made her happy. She liked to wake early, far earlier than Drew, make coffee, then curl up on the chaise and watch the sun break the horizon. She'd never grown tired of it until that fateful day. Nobody could predict what would happen next, but it had changed Chris forever—and changed Drew even more.

Hell hath no fury like a woman scorned.

Chris set the cup of coffee on the side table then took a

seat on the chaise. She sipped her coffee as she looked out over the mid-day sky. What had once been a magical place in a magical life was now only sad and bitter memories.

From downstairs, she heard the chimes of the grandfather clock. It was noon, and Drew's flight would land in Greensboro soon. The drive to Danville would take another hour, though. He would be back from the conference, back to the real world, and back to hear the latest news. His girlfriends were gone, and soon enough, he would be too.

The plan was set, and there was no turning back, not that Chris wanted to anyway. Drew had received plenty of chances to change his disgusting ways, yet he never had.

I'm sure he shared his bed in New York with plenty of women, too, ones he'll never see again. For that matter, he'll never see any other woman again. The last face Drew will ever see is mine—the way it should be. I'm still his wife, and I'll happily kill him in the home we shared for over twelve years.

Chapter 35

I couldn't wait to get back to the police station. I didn't know why they didn't investigate with any urgency, although nothing pointed a finger at a local resident as the killer. Our presence—and the similar murders in other cities—all but proved that. It didn't help that the only witness who had come forward days later was an autistic teenager who had cried wolf one too many times, according to the PD.

I tapped my laptop keys as Renz drove. I didn't know where our killer lived, so searching the local DMV records for a red Jeep could be a waste of time, but I had to start somewhere. I didn't have a year, model, or plate number, yet we had been in that position before and still came out successfully on the other side.

"Shit, Renz, this isn't going to be easy. Do you really think Tyler saw a woman?"

Renz nodded. "I do, and we were beginning to lean that way ourselves. The word 'slut' carved into the victims' cheeks seems more like something a woman would do."

"Wow. Can you imagine the egg on the police department's faces if Tyler actually gave us the lead we needed to crack this case?"

"They had the same opportunity we did. Actually, more. Even before Tyler came forward, it didn't sound like they were doing a lot of investigating."

I needed to focus on my laptop and the search for a red Jeep. "Too bad we don't have a model or a year to plug into the system."

"Forget the Jeep for now. Let's focus on the woman. Deena and Lorraine didn't know each other. We still don't have a name for the dumpster victim. Come to think of it, did you look at the most recent reports?"

"Not yet, but I should do that now before I forget to. Wait a minute!"

"What?"

"Tyler said he was walking in the same direction as the Jeep. He saw the red color when the alley streetlight illuminated it in front of him."

"Right."

"So, if he was walking behind the Jeep, he'd have seen the license plate too."

Renz frowned. "Wouldn't he have told us that?"

"Not necessarily. I don't know a damn thing about autism except that some kids can be savant like. Maybe they only answer specific questions that are asked, and we didn't ask him that."

"Call the house and find out before he leaves for work. Ask him if he saw the rear plate and remembers any of the numbers."

I snapped the locks of my briefcase and opened it then removed the copy of Tyler's statement. The phone number was listed on the report. I checked the time and made the call.

Mr. Spencer answered the phone on the third ring.

"Mr. Spencer, it's Agent Monroe. I need to ask Tyler one more question that I'd forgotten to earlier."

"He's about to head out the door."

"It won't take but a minute, I promise."

"He gets upset when he's late."

That comment made me wonder why the father didn't just drive Tyler to work, but that wasn't the issue.

"Please, Mr. Spencer. People's lives are at risk."

"Fine."

I let out a relieved breath when, a second later, Tyler came to the phone.

"Hello?"

"Tyler, it's Agent Monroe again."

"Yeah."

"Remember when you told us you saw the color of the Jeep when it passed under the alley lamp?"

"Yeah."

"That means you were walking behind it, right?"

"Uh-huh."

"Okay, good. Do you remember seeing the license plate?"

"It had a light on it, so yeah."

"That's great to hear. Do you recall any of the numbers on the license plate?"

"Yeah."

"And what were they?"

"A22-4981."

"You remembered the whole plate number?"

"Yeah, I'm good at remembering numbers."

"You certainly are. Thank you, Tyler."

I hung up and squeezed Renz's arm. "Holy shit, Renz. We're about to find out the killer's name." I tapped my computer keys and entered the plate number into the DMV's website. When the results popped up, I couldn't believe what I was looking at. "What the hell? I don't understand this at all."

Chapter 36

"I don't get why you're calling me, Chris. I got off the plane a half hour ago, grabbed my luggage, and now I'm driving home."

"It's urgent. I need to see you right away. You have to come to my apartment."

"Doubt that I will. I'm exhausted. Whatever you need to say to me, you can do it now over the phone."

"No, I can't. If you aren't at my apartment by four o'clock, I'm going to do something desperate. It'll ruin my life and your career, that's a guarantee."

"Are you threatening me?"

"No, but like I said, it's urgent."

Chris was getting through to him, and she heard it in his groan. He was about to give in if for no other reason than to shut her up.

"Fine, but I'm stopping at home first, taking a shower, then I'll grab something at a drive-through restaurant as I'm heading that way. Whatever it is you're going to tell or show me better be worth my drive."

"It will be. I promise."

With a grin, Chris hung up. Her plan had been put into motion, and Drew would be home soon. He would be irritated at having to deal with her that day when, in reality, Chris was sure all he wanted was to shower then head to his latest girlfriend's house for a romp in the hay. Little did he know that all of his girlfriends—at least the ones Chris knew about—were dead.

When he got home, Drew wouldn't expect to see her there. He would be rushed, pissed off, and wouldn't notice her until it was too late—the quintessential blindside and the one Chris looked forward to the most. She planned to knock him for a loop. Depending on how incapacitated he became, she would determine her next steps and the amount of time to take in prolonging his death.

Chris had already gotten Drew's favorite baseball bat from the garage. It would be a walk in the park to nail him in the face the second he crossed the door's threshold between the garage and utility room.

With the interior house lights off, just the way Drew had left them two weeks ago, Chris sat in the living room, peeked out between the slats of the blinds, and watched for his white Mercedes to come down the street. It didn't take long before it turned the corner a half block away and approached the house. Chris heard the overhead lift. She rushed to the utility room, picked up the baseball bat, and got ready to swing.

Seconds later, she heard the car door open and close. The trunk was next—he was grabbing his luggage. The trunk lid slammed, and she knew he would be at the door any second.

Drew would have his hands full, making his entry

awkward and clumsy. That would give her the perfect chance to catch him off guard. When Chris heard his footsteps, she stared at the doorknob and waited. In position, she raised the baseball bat, and as soon as the door opened fully, she would swing with everything she had and hope for a home run.

Chapter 37

Renz clicked the right blinker and pulled to the shoulder. "What is it? What don't you understand?"

"The Jeep is registered to Drew Mills, the cosmetic surgeon from Danville."

"Wait. What?"

I turned my laptop toward Renz. He stared at the screen, compared the plate number I'd typed in with the results, and confirmed that Drew Mills owned the Jeep. "How is that possible? His office told you he was at a conference in New York during the last two weeks."

"Maybe he wasn't really there. Saying you're somewhere else is always the perfect alibi for a crime."

Renz nodded. "It wouldn't be hard to confirm, so why take that chance? Why kill those women?"

I pressed my temples as I thought. "We need to do a deep dive into Drew Mills. One thing for sure is that his office isn't open today. They did tell me he would be back at work come Monday, though. That means he's either back from New York, will be coming home today or tomorrow, or never went at all."

"Pam mentioned that Lorraine's secret boyfriend had a white Mercedes, and Edna confirmed that."

"Right," I said. "Pam also said she followed Lorraine to Danville, where she saw her with a man." I put the computer back on my briefcase tabletop and tapped the keys.

"Now what?"

"Now, I want to see if Drew Mills also has a white Mercedes."

"You don't have a plate number to enter," Renz said.

"Well, then call Taft. We need to update her anyway, and she can have Tech pull up everything there is to know about the guy, including all the vehicles he owns."

Renz made the call to Maureen's cell phone since we weren't sure she was in the office on a Saturday afternoon. When she answered, he gave me a nod and set the phone to Speaker.

"Hello, Lorenzo. What have you got?"

"Hey, Boss, I'm calling with an update and a new discovery."

"Sure, go ahead."

"Jade and I interviewed the witness in Lynchburg, who happens to be autistic. His statement didn't hold a lot of weight with the PD there, but after talking to him, we learned that the person he saw was a female, the vehicle was a red Jeep, and he actually memorized the plate number. It comes back to Drew Mills, that plastic surgeon from Danville."

"That's a significant discovery, Lorenzo. What do you need from me?"

"We need everything the team can find on the man, including all other vehicles. We were told by his office that he was in New York at a conference for the last few weeks. That's why we dropped looking at him as a person of interest, but now, under the circumstances…"

"Right. Do you think he used the conference as a guise to commit the crimes?"

"Possibly. What would put a nail in his coffin is to find out if he owns a white Mercedes. We don't have a year, model, or plate number, but I'm sure Tech can find all that out. Supposedly, Lorraine Tilley was dating a man with a white Mercedes, but she was very secretive about him. Pam didn't know his name, but she did follow Lorraine to Danville, where she met up with a man."

"Do you know the whereabouts of Drew Mills right now?"

"No. All we were told by his office staff is that he'll be at work on Monday. That means he's either already home, heading there, or will be back in Danville sometime tomorrow."

"Okay, I'll get Tech started now. I'll do what I can to get a judge on the phone to issue a warrant for his home and that Jeep. Where are you now?"

"We just left Lynchburg and were planning to go to Danville anyway to search Deena Norman's home. Rita gave us permission to go inside. It's about an hour and ten minutes from our location right now."

"Yep, and I'll get back to you as soon as I can. Go through Deena's house, see if there's anything there that could lead to Drew Mills, then find out where he lives and drop an anchor within sight of his home. Stay in Danville until you hear back from me."

"Got it. Talk soon." Renz clearly noticed the frown on my face. "What's on your mind?"

"It still doesn't make sense."

"Which part?"

"The part where Tyler saw a woman with a ponytail get out of the Jeep, dump whatever she had slung over her shoulder, then climb back into the Jeep and speed away."

Renz scratched his chin as he sighed. "Yeah, it doesn't make sense unless—"

"Unless Drew Mills had an accomplice who committed the murders."

"Right, but what's the motive?"

I huffed. "That, my friend, is what we get paid to find out."

Chapter 38

Just over an hour had passed since Renz ended the call with Taft. We reached Deena's home in Danville, and what stood out the most was how sparsely populated the neighborhood was. Because each home was a good distance from the next, if a crime did happen in Deena's house, it was unlikely that anyone saw or heard a thing.

Renz parked in the driveway, and after getting out, we headed to the porch, where I lifted the third flowerpot and took a look under it. The key was right where Rita had said it would be.

I tipped my head toward the door. "Let's see if Deena's home holds any clues." I stuck the key in the doorknob and gave it a turn. Renz and I walked in, then I flipped on the light switch. We stood in a small tiled foyer. I looked around and didn't notice anything amiss. Just beyond the foyer was what was likely the family room. As we walked, we took in the surroundings and looked for any signs of a struggle. The home, although stuffy smelling, looked completely normal and clean. I was sure the mailbox was jammed full just like Lorraine's had been, but we planned to check that on our way out. Rita had mentioned that she would stop the mail delivery as soon as she arrived in town. I entered the kitchen and checked the garbage—nothing. I took a look in the washer and dryer. The dryer was full of clothes, and my assumption was that Deena never had the chance to empty it before she was killed. That led me to believe that either she was killed in the home or she'd rushed out under false pretenses to meet with her murderer.

We walked down the hallway and found what I'd hoped to see—a home office. I took a seat at the desk and opened the drawers. Because Rita had given us permission, we didn't have to play by the "look but don't touch" rules.

"I better grab some gloves out of my briefcase if we're actually going to go through things."

Renz nodded. "We aren't going to be here long, though. We've got to put eyes on the Mills house."

I returned to the car, opened my briefcase, and took two pair of gloves out of it. As I walked to the house, I noticed something odd at the flower bed.

I called out through the half-opened door. "Renz, come out here for a second."

He poked his head out the door. "What's up?"

I pointed at the void in the flower bed. "Doesn't that seem odd to you? A pretty large rock is missing for no reason?"

"I'm sure there's a reason, and it probably has something to do with that rock Deena was weighed down with."

I groaned with the realization that Renz was right. It was another clue that Deena might have been murdered in her own home.

"We're going to need a forensic team out here to Luminol this house," I said as I gloved up. "Meanwhile, I need to look through that desk."

Back in the house, while I worked in the office, Renz searched all the other rooms. If any clues were to be found, I was sure they would be in there. In the top center drawer was Deena's checkbook. I flipped through the register but didn't see anything of interest. I assumed most people put their bills on autopay or that they used a credit card for purchases. I continued on. Minutes later, I found a stack of credit card statements. They were filed by month, and since we were in August, it would take only a minute to check back to the beginning of the year. January through May didn't stand out, but once I got to June, something caught my eye.

"What the hell?"

I looked through June then July. Both months showed payments made to Born Beautiful, the cosmetic surgery clinic that Drew Mills owned. I set them on top of the desk and continued on.

"Bingo!"

In front of me was a monthly planner with dates, times, and places written down, including BB. It seemed similar to the calendar I'd seen in Lorraine's kitchen. I stood and yanked my phone from my pocket.

"Renz, I need you in here right now."

His steps quickened as he headed down the hall.

"Find something?"

"Hell yeah, but I need your help. First, I found these." I handed him the credit card statements. "Notice the charges made to Born Beautiful. Now take a look at this." I handed him the planner. "BB is written down a number of times. That has to stand for Born Beautiful. Deena was a client of Drew's."

"Okay, we're getting somewhere."

"So, here's my cell phone. Scroll through those pictures I took of Lorraine's calendar and see if there's anything that could be interpreted as Born Beautiful, like an appointment date or something to that effect. Maybe even DM for Drew's initials."

"Got it." Renz took my phone and sat on the side chair along the wall. "So, what do you think it all means?"

"I'm not sure. Maybe Drew screwed up on cosmetic procedures they had done and they were going to sue him."

"Hmm."

"What?"

"That might be another reason their faces were destroyed. What if he was trying to erase evidence of the botched surgeries he performed on them?"

"Damn, that could be it."

"I got something, Jade."

"What?"

"On June fifteenth, Lorraine has BB noted and then again on August thirteenth."

"So they were both patients of Born Beautiful, but that still doesn't explain why Tyler saw a woman tossing Jane number three into the dumpster."

"It could. Maybe Drew did go to New York, which would be an important alibi for him. It would totally exonerate him from the murders, but he could know a large, strong woman who did the deeds for him for the right price. He might have told her to make the women unrecognizable."

"Something still seems off, though. Why would a woman he paid to do the deed carve his initials in the victims' cheeks? It would be like she was squealing him out."

"Yeah, everything is still a mystery. I'm texting Taft. I have to tell her that Deena and Lorraine were Drew's patients. We're going to need a warrant for his business account and patient files too."

"Okay, and while you do that, I'll check the missing persons database again for any newly entered person with the initials SM. Regardless, she's one of his victims, too, even if he wasn't the one wielding the knife."

It took only a minute to check the most recent entries in the database. When I typed in SM, I couldn't believe what I saw. A woman who had just been reported missing yesterday popped up on the screen. Her name was Susan Manning, and she was from Lynchburg. I groaned in anxiety.

"You've got to be kidding me! I found a new entry with SM initials. It's a woman who's a Lynchburg resident. Why hadn't anyone reported her missing before this?" I was irritated beyond belief.

"There has to be a good reason."

"Yeah, well, I'd like to hear it. Seriously, Renz, we were just there. I feel like all we're doing is wasting gas instead of solving this case."

Renz huffed. "And we aren't on the best terms with the Lynchburg PD." After sending Taft the text, he pocketed his phone. "Let me see the report."

I got up and let Renz have the seat I'd been on. "It has to be her. The missing woman has black hair just like Jane number three."

"Okay, let's contact the person who filed the report. We have to know why a week went by before Susan was reported missing." Renz stood and looked around the room. "I don't think there's anything else we need to do here right now. Let's drop an anchor at the Mills house, then you can make the call from the car."

"Hang on." I snapped off pictures of Deena's June and July credit card statements then closed the desk drawers.

Once outside, I locked the door and returned the key to the underside of the third flowerpot on the porch. After that, I took a picture of the flower bed where the missing rock should have been.

I nodded at Renz. "Okay, I'm ready. Let's go see if there's any movement at Drew's house, and hopefully, we'll get good news from Taft before long."

Chapter 39

We found Drew's neighborhood about three miles away. From what we could tell by the homes on his street, all the residents had money. Every house looked to be on at least an acre lot, Drew's included. Four white pillars flanked the front porch of his two-story mansion. The front yard had formal gardens, and a winding sidewalk ended at the ornate front door of the redbrick colonial home. I could only imagine what the interior and backyard looked like.

Renz drove slowly past the home, which appeared dark inside. He turned around at the end of the block then returned and parked across the street two houses away from Drew's. The oversized garage was visible, and that was all that mattered. We would sit there as long as Taft wanted us to, so we settled in.

I craned my neck as I looked out the windshield at his and all the other beautiful homes on that oak-lined street.

"Holy shit. Those are quite the digs, Renz. I guess I'd understand why he'd want to shut up disgruntled patients. He could be sued for everything he has."

Renz wagged his finger at me. "Don't get ahead of

yourself, Jade. That's only speculation between you and me. Honestly, at this point, we don't know jack shit. Everything comes down to getting warrants for his home, vehicles, and patient records. After that, everything should be as clear as mud."

I chuckled. "I hope it'll be clearer than that. Right now, I need to find out what I can about Susan Manning."

With my laptop open again and the missing persons site pulled up, I found the entry that had come in yesterday for Susan Manning. She had black hair, stood between five two and four, and weighed anywhere from one hundred fifteen to one hundred twenty pounds. Our Jane Doe fit within those parameters. The person who'd reported her missing was a Camille Fine, who also lived in Lynchburg. Even though I was irritated that we'd missed the chance to interview the woman while we were in Lynchburg, the phone call would have to do.

I gave Renz a thumbs-up. "It's ringing. You want to listen in?"

"Yep. Put it on Speaker."

I did, and after the second ring, a woman answered.

"Hello."

"Camille Fine?"

"Yes. Who's this?"

"I'm Agent Jade Monroe with the FBI. I have you on Speaker, and my partner, Lorenzo DeLeon, is listening in."

Renz introduced himself.

"We saw the recent missing persons report you filed with the Lynchburg PD for Susan Manning."

"That's right. I'm so worried, and I can't reach her anywhere. She's my neighbor and closest friend."

"Camille, we have an unidentified woman at the morgue in Roanoke who matches the description of Susan, although she was found dead a week ago."

"Are you talking about the dumpster woman?"

"I am."

"Nope, that can't be Susan. She left for Arizona last Saturday and wasn't scheduled to come home until Thursday. I filed the report yesterday because I haven't spoken with her or received any texts from her for several days. She isn't home, and I don't have a number for the friend she went to visit. Either way, Susan doesn't respond to the numerous messages I've sent her. She's supposed to host a charity function in town on Monday, and I can't find her anywhere."

From her voice, I could tell Camille was getting frantic.

"Okay, take a breath. Here are the statistics we have on our Jane Doe. Black hair, brown eyes, five foot four, and one hundred nineteen pounds. Would you say Susan matches that description?"

"Yes, but it's impossible that it's her. That would mean she never went on vacation, yet we communicated for four days before her phone went silent."

Renz took his turn while I kept my eyes on Drew's home. "Camille, we believe the killer took the phone. The Jane found in the dumpster didn't have a phone or a purse with her."

Camille cursed loudly. "Are you saying that for days, I communicated with a killer who I thought was Susan?"

"If all you did was text each other, then yes. That kind of thing happens often to throw people off timelines and to the fact that something is wrong."

"Oh my God, I think I'm going to be sick."

"Is there any way to identify Susan that the killer wouldn't know? She doesn't have tattoos or notable scars, and her teeth and face were damaged, so…?"

"Wait! She does have a notable scar on her scalp. She showed it to me last year when we were talking about childhood injuries."

"Okay, where exactly is it?"

"Um, it's above her forehead, about two inches into her hairline. When she was a kid, she cracked her head on a railing when she was skateboarding. It's pretty wide, and you can't miss it if you look in the right place."

"Great. Thank you, Camille, and we'll let you know if our Jane really is Susan. You have our deepest condolences no matter what."

Renz ended the call. "Now, we have to let Dr. Morgan know. He'll have to check that area of Jane's head. It's the best and fastest way we've got to ID her."

Renz's phone rang as he was about to make the call. "Go ahead and contact the coroner's office while I get this."

"Is it Taft?"

He looked at the screen, and with a nod, he answered.

I made my call short, got to the point, and asked the doctor to text me as soon as he took a look for that scar on Jane's scalp. I was excited to hear Renz's call with Taft and to find out if she was able to obtain warrants for Drew Mills' home, vehicles, business accounts, and the patient list. I waited as Renz talked, and when he fist-pumped the air, I knew the warrants had come through. He thanked our boss and hung up.

"Okay, Taft found a judge here who issued the warrants based on what we have so far. The evidence is iffy, but we have an eyewitness to the Jeep being at the location where Jane three was dumped. That gives us probable cause." Renz let out a relieved grin. "We're finally going to nail that bastard."

"So where do we pick up the warrants?"

"They'll be delivered to the Danville Police Department in ten minutes." He jerked his chin toward my phone. "Find the address and let's go."

According to the maps app on my phone, the police department was only seven blocks away. It would take only a few minutes to get there.

I hoped the documents would be ready to hand over as soon as we walked in. I didn't want to waste too much time with red tape since we needed to get back to the Mills house to begin our search.

"We're going to need help, right?" I asked as Renz drove. "We have to get into his office, too, and we can't let anyone give the staff a heads-up to remove patient files."

Renz turned left at the light and pressed the gas pedal to the floor. "We'll get help. Don't worry."

Minutes later, we arrived at the Danville Police Department and walked in. We hadn't been there before, and we didn't even know who was in charge on a late Saturday afternoon. Renz took the lead, introduced us, and said we were there to pick up warrants.

"Sure thing, Agent DeLeon. Captain Morris is expecting you. It appears that an SSA Taft from the FBI's Serial Crimes Unit took care of everything. Give me one minute to let him know you've arrived."

Renz gave the officer a nod, and we waited. I checked the time on my watch and hoped he would be out soon. After another minute, footsteps sounded from down the hallway. I watched, then a fifty-something man appeared. He looked concerned yet had friendly eyes. He approached, introduced himself, and handed three warrants to Renz.

"I have four officers I can spare. We run a smaller shift on weekends."

Renz raised his hands. "Four is fine. I'd like two to join us at the house and the other officers to watch the cosmetic surgery center. We'll call in extra agents from Roanoke, but for now, and to assist in the home's entry, I think we're good."

The captain told us the officers were waiting in their squad cars and ready to go. We thanked him and left.

With one squad car at our rear bumper and the other en route to the clinic, Renz and I headed to the Mills mansion.

After reaching the home, we went to the front door, and the officers flanked the sides of the house, where they watched for movement. The gate to the rear of the property was locked, and there was no way around the seven-foot wall.

Renz pounded on the door and yelled out, "FBI, open up! We have a warrant."

Chapter 40

We listened for sounds coming from inside but hadn't heard any. Renz yelled out again, and we waited, but nobody responded.

"Get the ram. We're going in."

Officer Conway ran to the trunk of his squad car and brought the ram to the front door. Renz and I stood back while he gave it a forceful swing. It took several tries, but on the third attempt, the thick wooden door flew open and bounced off the inside wall.

We yelled out again as we made entry. One by one, we cleared rooms. The officers headed upstairs while Renz and I stayed on the main level. He went left, and I went right. Soon, I saw something abnormal. Cautiously, I approached the door that separated the laundry room from the garage. It was ajar, and what appeared to be dark spatter on the white doorframe told me nothing good had taken place there.

I yelled out to Renz, and he quickly showed up at my side.

"What have you got?"

I pointed at the spatter. There was no mistaking the nearly black color—it was blood.

We approached with our guns aimed at the dark opening. Once there, I reached into the garage and swatted at the wall until I hit the light switch. Other than a white Mercedes parked in the third stall, the garage was empty.

Rhetorically, I asked where the red Jeep was. Renz looked at me and shrugged. A minute later, both officers joined us at the door. They had finished clearing the second floor.

"Nobody is upstairs." Officer Conway pointed his chin at the doorframe. "What's that all about?"

"Looks like a crime scene to me," Renz said. "The question is, who does that blood belong to and where is Drew Mills?"

My phone rang, and I excused myself to the living room. We needed to back away from that blood anyway, get a forensic team en route from Roanoke, and find out if agents had been called to pitch in. It looked like we had a killer on the run.

I answered my phone to find Marty Trent, our FBI tech lead from Milwaukee, calling.

"Marty, what have you got?"

"Jade. We did a deep dive into everything Drew Mills related and found something interesting."

My ears perked up at that comment. "Yeah, like what?"

"Like a marriage license from 2010 to a Christine Campagna. The weird thing is we couldn't locate divorce papers. It appears that Drew Mills is married, yet there's nothing anywhere, not even a tax return, in that woman's name."

My head was spinning. "No credit cards, vehicle registration, cell phone bill, and you looked under the married name and the maiden name?"

"Yep, nothing there, but his business account has reoccurring payments to Riverview Capital Holdings."

"What the hell is that?"

"Would you believe apartment complexes, yet the only one located in Virginia is in South Boston."

"And that's how far from Danville?"

"About forty minutes east."

I tapped my phone's maps to find the location of South Boston. "Hmm… it's also about halfway between Clarksville and Danville. Okay, thanks, Marty, and keep digging. That woman has to be somewhere, maybe even in South Boston." I hung up and rushed to the laundry room and found Renz and the officers looking through the garage. "Marty from Tech just called. I think we have something."

"Yeah, same here," Renz said. "Blood smeared on the driver's-side visor of the Mercedes."

"Let me guess, the overhead garage door remote is gone."

"Ding, ding, ding. Give that woman a gold star." Renz popped the trunk, looked in, then closed it. "So, what did you find out?"

"That we may be looking at the wrong person."

Renz's eyes bulged. "Okay, we better go find a place to sit down. I want to hear everything Marty told you." Renz looked at Conway. "Tell those other officers to make entry into the clinic. I have a feeling we're going to need that patient list now. Also, get a forensic team out here right away."

We headed into the living room, where Renz took a seat across from me on the couch. I sucked in a deep breath then repeated everything that Marty had told me. "Drew was, and is, married, but the wife is unaccounted for. There isn't anything in her name. Not a vehicle registration, credit card, or even a tax return."

"Maybe he killed her too."

"Shit. That could be her blood on the doorframe. Marty said a payment goes out every month from Drew's business account to a Riverview Capital."

"Which is?"

"An apartment conglomerate, but there's only one complex in Virginia—in South Boston."

"A hideout? A place where he does his killing?"

"I don't know, but I think we better find out. I don't even know what the actual apartment complex is called. That name is the umbrella company's title."

"Okay, we need to get all our ducks in a row. Half of the agents should meet the officers at the clinic. Forensics has to go through this entire house from top to bottom, and Conway and Jessup need to stay here until Forensics arrives. The captain needs to send other officers out here to cordon off the street." Renz turned to Conway. "Can you take care of that?"

"You bet, sir."

"Great, then I'll have the other agents meet us in South Boston. We'll find that apartment complex and, with any luck, Drew Mills too."

With a plan set and Taft updated, we headed east. It could

take hours to locate the right building then the right apartment number. I doubted that anyone would be in the rental office at night either. While Renz drove, I searched for all of the apartment buildings in South Boston.

"Humph."

"What?"

"Well, we might get lucky simply because South Boston is a small town. My search shows ten apartment complexes, but I don't know how old that information is."

"Ten is better than twenty."

I grinned. "No shit, dummy."

A text came in on Renz's phone, and he asked me to take a look. "Who is it from?"

"Taft. She says two agents are heading to South Boston to pitch in."

"And the other agents?"

"Yep, another two will meet the officers at Born Beautiful. We should have confirmation within a few hours about the women on Drew's recent patient list." I sat quietly for a minute and thought.

Renz apparently noticed my silence. "Something on your mind?"

"Yeah. The whole wife thing is leading us down a different path. It still doesn't explain who Tyler saw getting out of and then back into the red Jeep. Maybe Drew and the wife are a killing team. Maybe the woman was her."

Renz raised his brows. "Anything is possible, Jade, and that would explain what Tyler described, but she'd have to be big and strong to heave a hundred-twenty-pound woman over her shoulder. There is the chance that Tyler didn't actually see what he thought he saw."

I groaned. "Well, something nasty is going to hit the fan and soon. I can feel it in my bones."

Chapter 41

By the time we had passed the city limits sign for South Boston, it was five thirty. I had spoken with Agent Tim Banks during the drive and arranged for him and Agent Carl Donahue to meet us at the gas station just before the Riverside Inn. He said they would be there in twenty minutes. That gave Renz and me just enough time to use the facilities and grab coffees and prepackaged sandwiches before they arrived.

We would gather somewhere, I'd print out the addresses of the buildings, and we'd divide them up. The best we could hope for was to see the red Jeep parked at one of the apartment complexes. That would narrow down our search considerably. If we didn't spot it, we would have to go to each location tomorrow during business hours and ask someone in the management office about their tenants.

It was six o'clock when Renz spotted a black SUV pulling into the gas station driveway. He nudged me with his elbow. "That's got to be them."

I downed what was left of my coffee, popped a breath mint into my mouth, then tossed my trash into the garbage can. By then, both men had exited the vehicle. Renz headed toward them and called out their names, and they responded with handshakes for both of us.

"So, how are we going to do this?" Banks asked. "Do we know exactly who we're looking for?"

"Not one hundred percent," Renz said. "There's a chance we're looking for a husband-and-wife killing team, a husband who is holding his wife hostage or has already killed her, or—"

"Or what?"

"Or a woman whose role we aren't sure of. The wife goes by either Christine Campagna or Christine Mills. The husband is Drew Mills, and they've killed three women that we know of. Or at least one of them has. Two of the women have been positively identified, and the other, we should know about by tomorrow."

I took my turn. "I did an online search and found ten apartment complexes in South Boston. The best we can do at this hour is to divide them up and search the parking lots for a red Jeep."

"What if they have garages?"

I sighed. "We'll be continuing tomorrow during business hours anyway, and we can talk to the management staff. The apartment is paid for through Drew Mills' business account, but they should still have a tenant name on file. We'll need to ask, yet finding that red Jeep parked in one of those lots tonight will reduce our workload tomorrow substantially."

"Sounds like a plan," Donahue said.

"Good. Let's see if that hotel next door has a business center where I can print off the apartment addresses. You guys take five, and we'll take five and see where that leads us."

With a nod, the agents returned to their SUV, and Renz led the way to the Riverside Inn parking lot.

Inside the hotel, and given complimentary use of their business center, I pulled up and printed off the names, phone numbers, and map locations of each apartment building in South Boston. After dividing them up according to proximity to each other, I handed Donahue the sheets on five of them nearest the north side of town, and we took the rest.

"What we're looking for is a red 2017 Jeep Cherokee. If you spot it, call or text us with the location, and we'll do the same if we see it."

On the top sheet, I had written down my phone number for the agents. With that, we parted ways, and I hoped for the best. In the car, I called out directions as Renz drove through town. At each location, we checked curbside parking, the apartment parking lots, and the spots in front of garages. We struck out on the first two complexes and continued on to the next.

I sighed as I led Renz to the third apartment complex. "You know that Jeep and whoever is driving it could be anywhere—at a grocery store, at a diner, at a gas station. Just because we don't see the Jeep parked at an apartment building doesn't mean it's the wrong place."

"True, but think of tonight as mostly a preliminary search for the vehicle. Tomorrow, we'll learn a lot more."

The third building was a bust too—no red Jeep, at least not at that moment. Renz pulled out of the lot and continued on. A text alert came across my phone as he turned left.

"This might be something." I tapped the text icon and read it aloud. "Yep, it's from Donahue, and they spotted a red Jeep. I'll text him the plate number to be sure."

With the text sent, Renz pulled off the road temporarily while we waited for confirmation. Afraid to blink, I stared at my phone's screen and watched for a response. The text came, and I fist-pumped the air.

"Yes! It's the right vehicle. He says they're at the Parkside Commons."

"Okay, how far is that from here?"

I typed the name into my maps app and checked. "It's three miles north of us."

"Tell him we'll be there in ten minutes."

"Got it."

Renz took off. We finally had a location where Drew Mills was doing whatever it was that Drew Mills did. Was that apartment his killing field? That seemed far-fetched. Apartments had thin walls, and unless he utilized an end unit on the ground level, dragging, carrying, or forcing a woman into that apartment against her will didn't seem possible without alerting the neighbors. One way or another, we would find out in the morning unless we were lucky enough to spot a directory with the tenant's name and apartment number listed on the wall by the entryway.

We arrived at the apartment complex just before seven o'clock. Renz pulled up to the rear bumper of the black SUV parked at the curb and killed the engine. We approached the driver's side but stayed out of view of the actual building.

Banks lowered his window and gave us a head tip.

"Where's the Jeep?" Renz asked.

"Halfway down the lot. It would have been nice if it was parked in front of a numbered garage, but it isn't."

"Any tenant directory?"

"We haven't left the vehicle. This is your investigation, so you two are the lead agents."

"Appreciate it," Renz said, then he turned to me. "Jade, you and I will go to the main entry and check it out. Donahue and Banks, why don't you casually walk up to the Jeep and see if you can gather any information from it?"

"Sure thing."

The four of us headed out, Renz and I to the front entry and Donahue and Banks to the parking lot.

Just beyond the covered porch was a glass door that entered into a vestibule. I pressed my face against the door, peered through it, and saw a directory mounted on the wall. "Let's check it out."

Renz and I entered and took a look. The directory showed the apartment numbers with a buzzer located next to each one. No names were listed.

"Damn it," I whispered. "We can't buzz each one and ask for Drew or Christine. That would take the element of surprise away and likely put someone at risk."

"Let's do a computer search for Drew Mills or Born Beautiful Inc. listed for Parkside Commons. There's nothing more we can do until tomorrow. We'll use the warrant for the company's records if the management person is uncooperative."

With a plan in mind, we headed to the vehicles and waited for the Roanoke agents to join us. Meanwhile, I searched the internet for Drew's or his company's name for Parkside Commons. Nothing came up.

"Damn it. I'm hitting a brick wall with this."

"We'll pick up the investigation in the morning as soon as the management office opens."

I looked out the passenger window, and our agents were walking toward our vehicles. According to Donahue, who had peeked through the Jeep's windows, the vehicle was relatively clean inside. Not even dust on the dashboard, he'd said.

I huffed. "It's probably been wiped down inside. How about the interior's back?"

"Tinted windows. Can't see shit."

I shook my head. "I guess we're at a standstill until morning, then. You guys up for staying in South Boston for the night?"

"Sure. We'll help you see this through until the end," Banks said.

I smiled. "I like you guys. Now, how about supper and a couple of beers?"

Chapter 42

After eating, we checked into the Riverside Inn, the same hotel where we'd used the business center earlier. We decided on a few drinks before calling it a night. At the far end of the bar, away from the other patrons, Renz and I ran different scenarios past the other agents.

We saw occasional nods as they listened to our theories.

Donahue spoke up first. "I'd say it's a killing couple even though the face carvings don't make sense. Maybe they like to create riddles for law enforcement to chase."

"That's a possibility," I said.

Banks spoke up. "And to substantiate his alibi, the wife took over when the husband was at the conference. If she's an invisible helper without a single account or a paper trail that leads to her, then it makes perfect sense."

Renz's phone rang. After checking the screen, he said it was Taft. He excused himself to a more private area since a couple had bellied up to the bar, only feet away from us. It didn't take long for Renz to return, and from the look on his face, I saw that something was wrong. He motioned with a head tip for us to join him at a bar table away from everyone else.

"What's wrong?" I asked.

"Well, that phone call confirmed more than we thought."

"Meaning?" Banks asked.

"Meaning the other agents entered the cosmetic surgery office with warrant in hand and pulled the client files. Every Jane that we've identified was a patient of Drew's." Renz paused. "Including Ruth Bedford."

I coughed into my hand. "Hold up. Lorraine had a secret boyfriend, and so did Ruth. We don't know anything about Susan Manning because her identity hasn't been confirmed yet. Maybe Deena had that same secret boyfriend. The white Mercedes and the fact that Pam said Lorraine met up with the boyfriend in Danville points more and more to the mystery man being Drew. Maybe none of the women were disfigured, but instead, Drew was juggling too many women at once and had to get out of his predicament, especially since he was still married."

"So, he enlisted the help of his wife, the woman he was cheating on?" Donahue asked. "That doesn't make sense."

I huffed. "Neither does the fact that there's blood on the wall at the Mills house. Somebody did something nefarious there. What we don't know is who the perpetrator or the victim was."

Renz checked the time. "It's getting late. We need to see if Parkside Commons has a website and if they do, what time the office opens in the morning. We'll be there at that time. Hopefully, the Jeep will still be parked there, and we'll find out once and for all what happened and to whom. As soon as we have the tenant's name and the unit they're in, we'll storm that apartment. For now, I think we should call it a night."

I told Banks and Donahue that I would text them the time to meet in the morning. With that, we said good night and retreated to our rooms.

I sat at the small table, my laptop in front of me, and found a website for Parkside Commons. Their rental and management office opened at eight o'clock. After texting that information to everyone and saying to meet downstairs at seven a.m., I put on my pajamas, texted a good night to Amber, and turned off the light.

I couldn't wait for the morning. We were so close, and finally, we would know who had brutally disfigured and murdered four women. I also needed to know the why.

Falling asleep wouldn't be easy, but I would do my best to shut down my thoughts, relax, and drift off. Tomorrow couldn't come soon enough.

Chapter 43

As soon as my phone's alarm went off on Sunday morning, I leapt out of bed. After starting the coffee, I hit the shower. A five-minute rinse was all I needed. I would wash my hair that night since it took hours to dry.

My clothes for the day had been chosen before I went to bed. All I had to do was guzzle two cups of coffee, dress, apply a little makeup, and brush my teeth. I would be ready to meet the guys downstairs in twenty minutes. I wasn't the type who needed to primp for an hour before going to the grocery store. Life was too short for that nonsense. As long as I was showered, reasonably put together, and dressed, I was good to go.

After brushing my teeth, I checked my watch—6:52. It was time to head downstairs. After gathering everything into my briefcase and packing my go bag, I pocketed my phone, grabbed my stuff, and headed out.

We would eat breakfast and be on our way. From the hotel, Parkside Commons was a seven-minute drive.

Downstairs, the men had gathered in front of the restaurant's entrance. Banks and Donahue talked among themselves, and Renz was on his phone. I assumed he was updating Taft.

Minutes later, the hostess escorted us to a window-side table. Not giving the menu too much thought, we all ordered the morning special—a stack of pancakes, bacon, and hash browns. With two carafes of coffee to go along with our food, we were set.

We ate without talking. We knew the drill. We would speak with whoever was in the office, run several names by that person, then present the warrant if necessary. We were good for Drew's business accounts, and since the apartment was paid for by Born Beautiful, we were legally allowed to ask, and the manager was legally required to provide that information.

It was time to go. We settled the tab and headed for our cars. Renz followed Banks to the apartment complex, where we parked in the visitors' spots.

I breathed a sigh of relief on seeing that the red Jeep hadn't moved. It was still parked in the same place it had been last night.

We exited the vehicles, me carrying the warrant and the guys leading the way. The management office had its own door to the left of the main entrance to the apartments. Because he was the senior agent in charge, Renz took the lead.

Two women sat at desks inside the office. They glanced up, and looks of concern instantly covered their faces. It wasn't often that three men in sport jackets and slacks and a woman in business casual attire walked in together. We all had our badges at the ready if for no other reason than to show we were serious.

"FBI agents," Renz said. "We need to speak with whoever is in charge of tenant relations."

"Excuse me? What does that even mean?" the brunette asked.

"Ma'am, do you have a list of tenant names?"

"Yes, of course."

"Good. We need to see it. Also, are those vehicles parked in the lot attached to the tenants?"

"They are, but without a warrant, we aren't obligated to show you anything."

"Then it's a good thing we have one." I held it out for her to see.

"Who does that red Jeep belong to?" Renz asked.

The woman shrugged. "A lady who keeps to herself, so I don't know her name. The apartment is registered to the company on the warrant you just stuck in my face."

I frowned. "Are you angry about something?"

She rolled her eyes and said something about having a bad morning.

The other woman spoke up. "That tenant lives in apartment six."

"And that's where, and how many bedrooms is it?" Banks asked.

The woman pointed. "At the right end of the building, and it's a two-bedroom. Should the other tenants be worried? Are you going in there with guns drawn?"

"I'd ask the tenant next door to leave their unit for now if they're home," Renz said.

"That's Bob Ewing's apartment. He's already left for work."

Renz nodded. "Okay, good. Remain inside and stay off the phone."

Donahue spoke up. "I'll stay here until you make entry."

I took my turn before we walked out. "Each apartment only has one outer door, right?"

"That's correct."

"Okay, thanks." I tipped my head toward the vestibule. "We'll need you to unlock the hallway door."

The helpful manager got up, jiggled a ring of keys as she picked the right one, then joined us in the vestibule and opened the inner door.

"Thanks," Renz said. "Now stay in the office until we say otherwise."

Renz, Banks, and I entered the hallway and turned right. Silently, we walked to the end of the corridor, where the number six was attached to the door. Renz whispered for Banks to stand on the right of the door, me on the left, and he would give it a hard kick. Since we already had the warrant in hand, we could yell out as we entered. A forewarning might end up with a bullet coming through the door.

Renz whispered again, and we drew our guns. "On my three. One, two, three."

With a firm boot to the door, Renz kicked it in, and I yelled out that we were the FBI with a warrant.

Upon entry, we didn't see anything other than a dark living room. The curtains were drawn, and the apartment appeared empty.

I yelled out again, "FBI, we have a warrant!"

It was eerily quiet—dead quiet. Banks turned toward the

kitchen. Renz and I headed down the dark hallway. Seconds later, Renz disappeared into the first bedroom. I took the one at the end of the hall, the master.

I heard him call out that he'd found a body.

The word *shit* popped from my mouth, but I continued on. I entered the master bedroom, and the bed was frumpy and unmade. I gave it a poke, but nobody was under the blankets. The en suite bathroom was just ahead, and even in the dark, a large body was visible, lying face down on the floor. The first thing I noticed was the ponytail. Could it be the same woman Tyler had seen? "Damn it." I knelt along the body to feel for a pulse. In a split second, she elbowed me in the face, flipped me over, and got me in a head lock. A knife was jammed against my throat, and my gun was spinning toward the shower stall. I stretched my arm and wiggled my fingers, but the gun was out of reach. I tried to kick and squirm, but it did me no good. My ability to breathe was being blocked by her elbow, and she was big and strong—stronger than most women.

She hissed in my face. "If I die, you die, too, cop. At this point, I have nothing left and nothing to live for."

I felt myself losing consciousness, and as everything around me went black, I heard the crack of a gunshot then the smell of gunpowder swirling around my head.

"Get her up and cuff her, Banks!"

The voice was familiar—Renz. I heard the call to 911 as I regained my bearings. I squinted and looked at my body. I had blood on my arm. Renz was asking for an ambulance, and I wondered if I'd been hit. Banks read someone their rights as the wailing sirens got closer.

"Jade, Jade, are you okay?" Renz asked.

I scooted back and leaned against the wall. "Yeah, I think so. Why is my arm all bloody? It doesn't hurt."

"It isn't your blood. It's hers. I'm not sure yet, but I assume she's Christine Mills. Drew Mills is dead in the first bedroom. His face is smashed in and carved up, but the ID in his wallet confirms it's him." Renz checked my neck. "Luckily, she didn't get the chance to slash your throat. I shot her in the shoulder before she took that deadly swipe."

My head was still spinning as I tried to make sense of what we'd walked into. I looked up, and Donahue and Banks had her restrained and sitting on the bed.

I cursed then asked who the hell she was.

"I'm Chris, but I'm sure you already knew that. So, who the hell are you?"

"My name is none of your damn business."

Seconds later, four EMTs walked in, stabilized her, and took her to a waiting ambulance. Donahue offered to escort her to the hospital while she was being treated then have officers take her to the local jail.

Before they took her away, I made sure she knew she hadn't seen the last of us. Renz helped me up, and we went to the first bedroom. I looked at Drew's lifeless body and tried to make sense of it.

"Maybe all of this is as simple as an act of jealousy."

"Maybe so, Jade. After all, it's one of the top reasons people commit murder."

Chapter 44

It wasn't until late in the day that we'd gotten word of Christine's move to South Boston's city jail. We were told she'd been treated for her gunshot wound, given painkillers, and was likely too groggy for a legitimate interview that would hold up in court. We would have to wait until Sunday morning.

Renz, Banks, and I had finished clearing the apartment earlier, had it sealed, then had Drew's body taken to the morgue in Roanoke, where the other bodies had been piling up.

We returned to Danville and began going through Drew's primary residence to see if we could find anything that confirmed or refuted our theory about him and Chris working together. We assumed she'd disabled him there, considering the blood we'd found on the doorframe, but why she took him to the apartment in South Boston was unknown.

Possibly, Chris had thought no one would find them there. She could take her time in killing him. If it was true that Drew and several of the women were having affairs,

Chris could have snapped and wanted to kill him slowly.

Of course, those were only my thoughts, and hopefully, we would get the truth out of her tomorrow.

We continued searching Drew's home. Since the house was large, it would take time, yet our best chance of finding anything of importance was likely in his office.

The three of us concentrated on the oversized room and dug in. Renz went through the desk, Banks through the file cabinet, and I took the oversized closet.

It didn't take long to find what I needed to put the puzzle pieces together. After I opened one of a half-dozen boxes that sat on the upper shelf, I called the guys over.

I took a seat on the floor and began going through hospital bills and receipts. I found another receipt for a funeral home, casket, and burial plot. Someone had died, and that might have been one of the triggers that set Chris off.

Renz opened another box and found hundreds of photos of Drew with women, and none of them were Christine. He was definitely a player and seemed to have been for years. Renz picked up a handful of photos and flipped through them. "Some of these pictures look to be from years ago, and others are more recent. Maybe this behavior is what led to his demise."

I stood and walked to the door.

"Where are you going? There's a treasure trove of information here."

"I need to go through the bedroom dressers and closets. I won't be long."

I walked upstairs to the bedrooms and entered the master

first. I opened the double-doored closet, and the light went on automatically. Inside, I found only men's clothing—suits, white button-down and casual shirts, dress pants, khakis, and jeans. Nothing in that closet belonged to a woman. I pulled open the dresser drawers and found men's undershirts, socks, and underwear. Again, nothing belonging to a woman. In the bathroom was a toothbrush holder containing one toothbrush. I left the master and entered another bedroom. A bed stood against the wall. The room was as immaculate as if it had never been used, and every dresser drawer was empty. The closet showed the same thing—nothing but three empty hangers on the rod. There were two more bedrooms upstairs, and both gave me the answers I was looking for. Christine didn't live in that house—no woman did. It was beginning to make sense. Christine was out, and Drew's fantasy of being a playboy with playmates was in. His home was a playground for him, and that was where he entertained a different woman many nights of the week. If he'd had a real girlfriend, she would have left a few personal items there, but the home was devoid of anything female. I was sure that was deliberate.

I returned to the office, where Renz and Banks were still looking at pictures.

"Find anything?"

"Yep. The answers I was looking for."

Renz dropped the photos back into the box. "And what was that?"

"Christine doesn't live here, nor does any other woman. This is Drew's lair. It's where he entertains different women. I'm sure it was at the clinic that he met Lorraine, Deena,

Ruth, and probably Susan. Chances are there are a dozen more women that Chris didn't know about or hadn't had the chance to kill. She and Drew weren't a team of bloodthirsty killers. She was a solo act."

Renz raised his brow then looked at Banks. "Sounds like Jade is onto something."

"It does to me too. Maybe Drew was meant to be Chris's final kill, and because they're still married, maybe she was hoping for a big payday as long as she didn't get caught."

I nodded. "And from the looks of the apartment she lives in and that five-year-old Jeep versus his brand-new Mercedes, he wasn't very generous with her either. I bet he had a prenup too. Essentially, Chris was out, and Drew's girlfriends were in."

"The question is why," Renz said.

"And that is the million-dollar question. Hopefully, we'll learn the answer if we get Chris to talk."

After putting the boxes back on the shelf, Renz closed the closet door. "I've had enough for the day. Let's head out. The apartment in South Boston is secure, and the clinic will be temporarily closed."

"So, all we need to know is if Susan and Jane number three are one and the same. Tomorrow, we'll interview Chris, and after that, we're heading back to Milwaukee." I looked at Banks. "You and your local team can take over the case."

Later, we sat down to a leisurely supper then retreated to our rooms early. I would shower, wash my hair, and relax in front of the TV while it dried. That was the night one of my favorite reality shows came on, and I missed it more often than I watched.

My phone buzzed in my hand. I nearly tossed it across the room before I realized that I had drifted off and it was simply a text coming in. I slipped on the reading glasses that I wore only when I was overly tired. The text was from Renz. He said the forensic lab had confirmed the scar on Jane's head. Susan Manning was our dumpster Jane, and now each victim had a real name attached. We would pass that information on to the Lynchburg PD, and they could gather DNA from Susan's house to submit to the crime lab for an absolute match.

With that bit of sad but much-needed news, I wrote myself a note to call Camille tomorrow and put her mind to rest. Susan, her neighbor and dearest friend, was dead.

I shut down the TV—another missed episode—and turned off the light. It felt good to close my eyes and sink into the pillow. I would be asleep in seconds.

Chapter 45

We had an interesting day ahead. It would be the typical wrap-up day filled with paperwork like we had done dozens of times in the past. Before transferring the case to the locals, we would interrogate Christine Mills. Interviewing criminals, if they chose to talk, was the part of my job I always found fascinating. Entering the mind of a killer to see what made them tick and why they committed their crimes always intrigued me.

Our interview with her was set for eleven a.m. That would give us time to have breakfast, organize our notes, and drive to South Boston, where she was being held in their city jail.

During the drive, I would call Camille and tell her the bad news. Susan Manning was the victim found in the Lynchburg dumpster. I'd also call Dani and tell her that Ruth was dead.

We met downstairs at eight o'clock, and the three of us had breakfast together. Banks would drive back to Roanoke alone. Donahue had returned last night with the other agents. Renz and I would head to South Boston, and when the interview with Chris was complete, we would return to

Roanoke, tie up any and all loose ends, then head to the airport, where we would board a late-afternoon flight to Milwaukee.

After breakfast, we said our goodbyes to Banks. It was likely we would see him and the other agents later. We would pass along the details of our interview with Chris, then the team at the Roanoke FBI field office would take over the case from there.

As Renz drove, I gathered my notes and questions for Christine. She could either lawyer up immediately or comply and tell us why she'd murdered five people. I was hoping for the latter. She definitely had a reason. It was possibly just the fact that Drew was a cheating husband, and from the pictures we'd found, it appeared that he'd been carousing for some time. The marriage license our tech team had found indicated that Drew and Christine had been married for over a decade.

I closed my eyes and saw the images carved in the women's cheeks. In hindsight, it all made sense. The initials identified each woman by name. The word "slut" was etched in their cheeks because that was how Chris viewed them. It could represent Drew in her eyes as well, and finally, she'd carved Drew's initials—and the initials of his occupation—on their faces. That told me she blamed him for her actions. I agreed with her reasoning, but murder was illegal no matter how many excuses one might use for committing such a heinous crime.

After I wrote down everything we would ask, I called Camille and gave her the bad news. I assured her there would also be a DNA comparison for definitive proof, but so far, it appeared that Susan Manning was dead.

We arrived in South Boston, and I called out the directions to the city jail, which was part of the police station complex. Renz parked, we entered and identified ourselves, then we were directed to the jail area, where we were told that Christine was being moved into an interrogation room. She hadn't asked for a lawyer. I'd found that more often than not, a murderer enjoyed talking about what they had done. Many times, they realized life as they knew it was over, they didn't have anything to live for or to lose, and they just wanted to tell their story. Unfortunately, many murderers didn't have a backstory—they killed simply because they enjoyed the power it gave them over their victim.

Renz and I sat in the viewing area to watch Christine for a few minutes before we entered the interrogation room. I realized just how large she was and how easily she could have ended my life. Even though she was sitting, I would have put Christine at six foot and close to two hundred pounds.

Watching her behavior before we walked in would be helpful in knowing how to approach the interview. We could appear sympathetic to get as much as possible out of her, go in with the good-cop-bad-cop personalities, or just go in and drill her for information. No matter what, we didn't want her to clam up.

She sat in the room, bellied up to the stainless steel table, and stared at her cuffed hands. Her shoulder was bandaged, and that arm was in a sling. She didn't look agitated or even angry. Her appearance was that of someone who had spent a sleepless night, possibly thinking of her actions and their consequences. I wouldn't let my personal feelings get in the way of my job. No matter what, and no matter if I felt sorry for her, Christine Mills was a cold-blooded murderer who'd held a knife to my throat, and if it hadn't been for Renz's quick actions and steady aim, I might have been one of Christine's victims too.

It was time to start the interview. Renz and I walked into the interrogation room. After the door closed at my back, she finally looked up.

She chuckled at the sight of us. "If nothing else, at least you stick to your word, Detective—"

"We aren't detectives. We're FBI, and our names aren't important right now. We were called in because we're part of the Serial Crimes Unit, and your victims were found in several states."

Chris's grin sent shivers up my spine. Maybe there wasn't a reason to feel sorry for her. I didn't know her or Drew's backstories, and it was possible that she was just as much to blame as Drew for the demise of their marriage.

"Well, aren't you special, Agent—"

"Like I said, our names aren't important to you."

Renz and I sat down across from her. I placed my folder of notes and cell phone photos and a pen next to me and out of her short reach. I wouldn't trust her with any sharp objects, and I'd known more than one person who had been stabbed with a pen. I set my phone to record our interview.

She looked long and hard at Renz. "You're the asshole who shot me."

"Guilty as charged," he said, "but you were about to kill my partner, so it was justified. What is it that has you so pissed, Christine? Who were you actually mad at? Was it Drew or the women he was juggling in his spare time? There had to be a trigger that made you lose importance in his eyes. How did that happen? What was the switch that flipped for him?"

"You don't know shit about my life, Mr. Agent Man."

"And that's why we're here. To try to understand what caused you to kill five people."

"Good thing you didn't say five innocent people because none of them were innocent."

I took my turn. "Are you sure none of the women were innocent? I mean, did they even know Drew was married? He could have spun a great story for each of them. Juggling four women takes a lot of time and focus. He couldn't slip up and call someone the wrong name, he had to put their dates on a calendar of sorts, and he had to keep the house sterile when they visited. Nothing sets a woman off more than finding another woman's personal effects in her boyfriend's house."

Chris pounded her fist on the table, and it vibrated against my legs. "They weren't that stupid. They knew he was married, and they probably knew he had multiple girlfriends. That was our house, my husband's and mine. I had life by the ass—money, respect, and a beautiful home. I thought it would be forever, but Drew was sickened by my appearance after—"

"After what?" I leaned in a little closer. "Tell us what Drew did, Christine. Help us understand."

Tears ran down her cheeks, and her voice caught in her throat. "We were going to have a baby. I was over the moon, but I could tell that Drew wasn't nearly as excited as I was. Looking back, I believed it ruined his image as a flirt, a hot, successful cosmetic surgeon, the man about town. Soon, he'd be a family man, not the man that every woman wanted and fawned over anymore. Women flocked to his clinic because he was good-looking and his promise of transforming all of them into beauties was intoxicating." Chris huffed. "That's exactly what he did, and then he bedded each and every one of them." She dipped her head and wiped her eyes. "Our baby didn't make it. Deep down, it was probably my fault. I was anxious all the time. When the baby came out stillborn, I went off the deep end. I had nothing to live for. I gained seventy pounds and went into a state of depression. Yet Drew's life carried on. He became verbally abusive and told me I was a fat, pathetic pig. He went out all the time, some nights not even coming home. I knew where he was, and I found out who he was sleeping with. My life spun out of control when he kicked me out. He said he was sick of having a useless, whining wife who didn't care about her appearance. The way he put it was that he didn't want to be associated with 'ugly' anymore. He constantly reminded me that when we met, I was a successful model who weighed one hundred twenty pounds and was beautiful, but now, I made him sick. I slashed the faces of those women because of him. He made them beautiful, yet I was still ugly in his eyes."

"But why now? What caused your bottled-up anger to explode?" I asked.

"Opportunity. Drew was out of state at a conference. I had the time, and I knew he wouldn't find out about the murders until he was back. I'm sure he called his ladies over and over again, but they didn't answer." She snickered. "That's because I killed the bitches."

I winced. At times, Chris saddened me, and at other times, I saw the evil that had been building inside her come out.

"Can you imagine the humiliation of being thrown out of your own house and having to live in a run-down apartment building with nobody who cared? Drew had a prenup when we got married, and unless we stayed together for fifteen years, I got nothing. He made sure that didn't happen, and nothing was ever in my name."

Everything Chris had said added up. Her husband was a jerk and a philanderer, but he didn't deserve to die because of it.

"You'll have to request a public defender since Drew's finances and accounts will be frozen during the investigation," I said. "You really don't have a chance at his money, and where you're going, you won't need any."

I looked at Renz, and he gave me a nod. I went to the secured door, gave it a knock to alert the guard, then went to the table and picked up the folder. There was no need to stick the pictures of Chris's victims in her face. She was coherent and well aware of what she did. We said goodbye and walked out.

We had a two-hour drive to Roanoke ahead of us. I would try to get most of the tedious paperwork done during the drive. Again using my briefcase as a tabletop, I filled out a hard copy of our interview with Christine to go in our files as well as the Roanoke FBI office's files. In a few days, I would email them a copy of our recorded interview too.

Having time in the car to wind down, Renz and I discussed normal everyday things. It was Monday, Labor Day, and college football was playing that night. I knew Renz was exhausted. Otherwise, I would have invited him to our house to watch the game.

"Hey, I know college football will already be on when we get back, but how about next Sunday for the start of the NFL season? I believe it's my turn to host a football party."

"Sounds great if we're in town."

"Taft promised to rotate us, remember? It's Charlotte and Kyle's turn to go out of town."

"Sweet."

"Sucks that we missed Jack's barbecue party today, but maybe there will be a pity package waiting for me when I get home." I leaned back in my seat and rubbernecked at the passing landscape as we made our way to Roanoke.

Our flight was scheduled to leave at four o'clock eastern time, and since it was nonstop, we would arrive in Milwaukee at five fifteen local time. Renz's car was in the airport parking garage, then we'd ride to our satellite office, where I could pick up my car and drive home. I was unlikely to walk through the door before seven o'clock.

After grabbing a drive-through meal and eating it during the last five miles into Roanoke, we arrived at the FBI field office at two p.m.

We had an hour to finish our paperwork, explain how the interview with Christine had gone, and leave the agents with the hard copy of the interview I had put together in the car. We thanked them for their assistance, then I left all my files with the photos of the women, the contacts at every police department we'd worked with, and our own contact information. We shook hands and wished them good luck.

"Don't forget, we're only a phone call or email away."

We headed out and had to return our rental before continuing into the airport and to our gate. I texted Amber as we waited to board and asked if they were home yet. She said they were still at Jack's house, but the party was winding down. They would definitely be home when I got there.

Chapter 46

Our flight was trouble-free and seemed to go quickly. I was sure that had something to do with the fact that the last thing I remembered was rocketing down the runway and taking to the sky. Renz had slept through most of it, too, based on the mouth smacking he was doing when the landing gear came down and jarred him. It woke me up and likely him too. I had seen him sleep before, and he was definitely a mouth breather.

Once we had landed, it took another twenty minutes to reach his car in the parking garage. Luckily, our office was only a few miles from the airport, and it would take less than ten minutes to get there.

"Guess this is it until Wednesday. It'll be nice to sleep in tomorrow," I said.

Whenever we spent time out of town, we were given the day off work on our first day back. It wasn't often we had the opportunity to use our vacation time, so Taft had implemented the bonus day off for all of us. I had to admit I enjoyed a day at home to wind down.

Renz dropped me off at my car, waited until I was safely

inside, then lowered his window. "Drive safe," he said as he gave me a wave.

I listened to my favorite classic rock channel as I drove the forty-minute distance home. I liked the time alone to reflect on the last week, the case, and its likely outcome. I was sure Chris would spend life in prison, and that was something I thought she'd accepted.

A smile crossed my face as I finally turned in to my driveway, waited as the overhead lifted, then pulled in. I lowered the garage door, grabbed my go bag from the back seat, and walked into the house.

I heard the football game and the whooping and hollering coming from Amber and Kate as they sat in the family room. I took in a deep breath and smelled what I believed to be barbecue ribs warming up in the oven. I tossed my go bag on the washer, headed to the fridge and cracked open a beer, then joined my sis and best buddy on the couch. The ribs would be warm enough to eat in ten minutes, and my pity package of party food was ready whenever I was.

Life was good, being home was great, but relaxing in front of the TV with my sweet sister and dearest friend couldn't be beat.

THE END

Thank you!

Thanks for reading *Blood Stream*, book six in the FBI Agent Jade Monroe Live or Die Series. I hope you enjoyed it!

Find all my books leading up to this series at http://cmsutter.com

Stay abreast of my new releases by signing up for my VIP email list at: http://cmsutter.com/newsletter/

You'll be one of the first to get a glimpse of the cover reveals and release dates, and you'll have a chance at exciting raffles offered with each new release.

Posting a review will help other readers find my books. I appreciate every review, whether positive or negative, and if you have a second to spare, a review is truly appreciated.

Find me on Facebook at
https://www.facebook.com/cmsutterauthor/

Printed in Great Britain
by Amazon